The Plum Explosion

The Plum Explosion

John van der Zee

Harcourt, Brace & World, Inc., New York

1000208

Copyright © 1967 by John van der Zee

Library of Congress Catalog Card Number: 67-10772

Printed in the United States of America

for Diane

Follow the fellow who follows a dream.

—OLD SAYING

Part One

Part One

I

Once the land was flat in a circle of ragged mountains.

Then a stream weighed it down with rock and silt until it sagged into a valley. Like cloth, the ground wrinkled. The folds drew closer to the sun and were bleached and baked, while the creases turned green and shady. Mud lingered; green shoots sprang from it. The mountains were worn round and overgrown with tawny grass that moved with the wind, like hair.

Nobody had been there yet. Except maybe an Indian.

Deer pushed paths to the edge of the creek; birds built nests in the bushes. Clusters of scrub oak appeared, green blotches on the hills. Tribesmen came with homemade snares and spears. They chased some animals; others chased them.

Then a Spaniard or Mex trooped over the horizon on horseback, waving a land grant, and on the sunniest, best-watered spot he built a rancho. He turned a few spavined cattle loose on the land, but food grew faster than they could eat it. And some Anglo came and took it away from him.

At last, a man came along in a wagon, old-country Italian, most likely, or perhaps a Portugee. He was the first to take a real look at what was underneath his feet. And when he broke the land, it fell in rich chunks to either side of his plow, black as acres of coal.

He planted row after row of green sprigs, and dug irrigation ditches, and set out a crop he knew he couldn't sow and reap in a single season. He'd come to stay.

His trees grew at the same rate, all in neat rows; he tended them when they were sickly, and that was a lot of work. And he tended them when they were well, and that was a lot more. He whitewashed their trunks, pruned their branches, harvested their fruit. They were his calendar.

For a long time, or what passes for a long time these days, you could see it all: hills the shape and color of sleeping camels around green rows of trees; winding roads built on deer and cow paths; the tame country and the wild.

It's all gone now. The land men hunted on and bought and stole and gardened is covered completely with cement and asphalt and rows of houses that grow all together like trees in an orchard, then stop, and age without ripening.

That the look of things has changed doesn't really matter much, because it's been changing all along. What's different now is that any feeling of intimate contact with the earth is gone. It could just as easily have been asphalt all along. And because of this sudden paving over of the past, the last fruit farmer who sat in his house watching Bonanza was closer to those first long-haired hunters creeping along making quail cries than to all the rose-tending, lawn-mowing, insecticide-spraying peace seekers who will occupy his land ever afterwards.

Which is, of course, until the next change comes.

Moss strode along a rank of trees and sighted down the files as though he'd uproot anything out of line.

Squinting in the sunlight, he picked out a low trunk with wide-spreading branches, ducked into its cool shade, planted his ass down on the smooth, dusty orchard floor and leaned back against the tree. Ah. Best way to scratch between the blades. Remove a pebble here, an old oblong plum pit there.

Now, got to memorize the history of the due process clause. Learn that mother backwards.

But before he got the textbook out of his lap, he was looking around, his face tensed, jaw stuck out, listening. He could feel the silence in there.

Fifty yards from a highway tide of cars, there was no highway noise. Instead there was a thick, cottony quiet, and in it he could hear frail sounds. Birds fluttered in the near trees and whistled in the distance; breezes flowed round the leaves. Moss listened. The dappled light moved and jumped through the branches; a squirrel scrambled up a trunk. Moss watched. Everything was moving and growing, just a shade too slow to see. But Moss could feel it. It was alive, but orderly, the way things ought to be. And the order of things soothed him. He leaned his head back and looked up through the green darkness at the sky. Bright light struck his eyes, and he blinked a few times, then closed the lids. The pointing face relaxed, and the uneven teeth parted, the jaw drooped, he slept; a long, angular man with big hands and feet and strawlike stick-up hair. A padded scarecrow. Flies buzzed around his head, ants scouted his feet. It was, he thought, clutching his law book in half-sleep, such a civilized place.

Moss didn't come to the orchard every day. Some days it rained or got dark early. Once there was a frost. And one afternoon he picked up a girl at the bookstore and shacked up with her. But he was fairly regular. It was mostly that he didn't like living all one way. The library was fine, but it was like class. Same dusty odor and closed-off view. Were they shutting in the students or shutting out the world? He was too old to hang around the campus. Without a coat and tie he couldn't pass for an instructor, and he wasn't about to dress up every day. The young, fresh faces gathering and talking on the campus corners looked right past him, and once a gardener shooed him away from a bicycle rack.

He often wished he were someone else, somewhere else.

He knew so few of the other students, and understood so little about them, that they seemed to him almost romantically remote. They were like the young people in magazines, standing around laughing at automobiles. All that smiling, all that laughter, all those "Hi!"'s. Whatever it was that college was supposed to be, those kids were wired into it.

And Moss, too old, was not.

He was alone, in a place that discouraged aloneness. Everyone was supposed to belong to something—frat, dorm, wing, room, dining hall, ball club, band, legal society, political party, drinkers. Even the bearded miscegenators, foreign students, and women once divorced got together for parties as a kind of campus underworld. Moss got together with no one. Oh, he met people, made acquaintances, fumbled through conversations with girls; but when he had a choice, he chose to be alone. And on a college campus, that is impossible.

Walk down a quiet, shady college street with the wind rattling dry leaves over the pavement and a tart autumn smell in the air; and as your lungs begin to clear and your taste and touch return and your body starts to transcend work and world, what happens? An iridescent-painted car, tires squealing, hangs the corner and comes rapping down that peaceable little street, shattering its sight and silence. And when the sullen-faced driver pulls even with you, he stops, motor rumbling and you almost into the gutter, and he gives you the finger. Or offers you a lift. And then peels out. Why can't he leave you alone? What have you done to him? You have reminded him of his own loneliness.

Moss tried walking along the highway, and felt that he was on display. He hiked for miles back of the campus and climbed a hill he hoped would have a view, only to find a college couple making out at its summit. By seeking places he thought he might like, he ran into others who liked them, too. He began looking for a place that no one else wanted, and that was how he found the orchard.

South a few miles from the school, the land was given over to fruit ranches so large the trees enclosed the highway with vast green walls. It gave things a private, forbidden look Moss liked. And one afternoon when it was autumn and hot, he turned his dingy '48 Frazer onto the highway shoulder, got out, and went exploring.

The air was heavy with the stale, sugary odor of ripening fruit; and the trees were as still and green as the water of a small inland lake. The branches were so thick with leaves and the ranks of trees so deep that Moss could see a greater distance into the countryside by bending over and sighting along the ground than he could standing up. Down the long tunnels of trees he saw no house and no people. Fruit had fallen in circles around the bases of the trees; the lower limbs were so heavy with ripe apples, apricots, plums, or pears that they had to be propped up with laths. From the highway it was difficult to tell where one owner's property ended and the next began. The only thing that changed was the signature scrawled on the paper NO TRESPASSING, NO HUNTING signs.

Moss walked along the shoulder until he came to an orchard that had a sign nailed to every tree facing the highway. He entered it. And in that cool, quiet solitude, among the forbidden trees, he found what he'd been seeking.

This is the place where I am me.

He picked a plum off the orchard floor and rubbed its purple haze away on his shirt sleeve, polishing it until it was a deep, true ruby. Then he slipped it into his shirt pocket and made footprints deeper into the trees. The signs, he found, could be ignored. They were put up by someone who thought a sign, like a gun, was all that was needed to make people obey. And after all, he'd come to take nothing. Only to see and feel.

The orchard was planted all in one crop, and plums hung thick on the branches or lay rotting on the ground, soft, purple, and juicy as giant grapes. Around each tree was a little mulch of dust, and some trees were sprinkled with a gray chemical powder. Certain trees were daubed with white paint. Others showed holes healed with mortar. The trees filed away in every direction as far as Moss could trace; yet no matter how closely he looked, he could see care. The place was tended like a garden, where no one ever strolled.

There wasn't a scrap of paper or a beer can or a discarded automobile tire in sight. Not even a set of footprints other than his own. At last, far down the aisle, he saw something shiny, a flash of light as at the end of a long tunnel, but brighter. Sun on a metal roof. Around a long, windowless wooden shed, weathered a furry brown, crates were scattered, some new, some gray with use. A small tractor, half covered with a tarp and hitched to a row of sharp, shiny discs, waited in the shade. Moss saw no one, heard no one; he sat on an empty crate to rest.

Near the busy city street on which Moss had grown up, there was and is a park where children still play tag and heats and hide-and-seek. Moss, from the time he was a toddler, had been the hardest of his crowd to catch. When a game began, the kids spread out in all directions and ran to hiding places where they crouched or sat trying to hold their bladders and their breath. But where the others stopped, little Raymond Moss ran on, leaping branches, diving deeper into the brush, tearing the knees out of his pants, skinning his elbows. He ran beyond the city sounds and the voices of his friends. He ran until the trees were too thick for him to walk; then he scrambled along the ground until the brush grew too thick to crawl. And there, in the deepest, thickest part of the park, so far away from the busy city that growing green things were closing in around him, Moss lay in hidden stillness and waited. And the feeling he had known then, a trembling, sweaty mixture of solitude and darkness, power and fear, returned to him as he sat in the quiet plum orchard.

They can't get me here.

His sweaty clothes turned cold on him, and he began to feel sore and stiff. He stood and circled around back to the highway, got lost twice, and came out of the orchard more than a mile south of where he'd parked his car. The highway's noisy chaos struck him as though he'd just come up from under water. And he knew he'd return the first chance he got.

Through that fall, Moss came to the orchard almost

9

daily, feeling now and then like a pagan tree worshiper. Sometimes he studied, but mostly he walked, or slept, or watched.

Because his pastime wasn't shared, like skiing or chess, he felt guilty about it. He began to check for anyone watching when he parked beside the orchard, and he always brushed the mud off his pants when he left.

The orchard was different every day; sometimes low clouds passed over as swift as smoke, or a branch lay broken, fresh and white at its fracture like turkey meat. The light changed, and in the mornings there was dew. It seemed to Moss that if he could just look close enough, he would see some fundamental movement of nature. And then be struck blind or dead.

One December afternoon, when the sky was gray and heavy as cement, Moss left his stuffy room, bailed out, and floated like a parachutist down over the rows of trees, was caught and dangled, then freed, and dropped softly and silently to the ground.

There were no birds that day, no fruit, not even any leaves. Just gray trunks and bare branches and little piles of cuttings. Far down a line of trees a workman in blue coveralls stood on a ladder and pruned branches. And the only sound in the orchard was the steady clip of his shears. He seemed no more a part of what was really happening among the trees than a plasterer working quietly in a cathedral.

If the clipping sound had stopped, and he had closed his eyes and turned around, Moss knew he wouldn't be able to find the man again down the long rows of trees. Seeing him, hearing him, he couldn't be certain he was there at all. The thought frightened Moss and excited him. For a moment he wanted to see the man up close, look at his face, talk to him. And then he knew he shouldn't.

Instead, he walked among the bare trees at a distance from the man with the shears, carefully keeping him in sight and listening for his clipping noise. He could get lost otherwise.

And so Moss went from class to the orchard to his stark, clean, cramped room. His grades improved and his money lasted a little longer. He drank less and slept better. He was hardly ever bored. And he shared his life with no one.

He read Thoreau and Walt Whitman. And reread them. And then books on trees, soil, flowers. The ones he liked, he bought and kept in his tiny room. When he could afford it, he bought them new.

"Aw. You're buying *Walden*."

A smooth, throaty voice had picked him out of a bookstore crowd. It belonged to a tall, soft-looking girl with light brown hair who wore butterfly-frame glasses that looked as though they were about to fly off her nose. She took the book right out of Moss's hands.

"Beautiful man. I love him."

"No future in that," said Moss; "he's dead." He took the book back firmly.

Shapeless in a gray coat, she followed him to a counter where a pimply clerk rang up the sale, then on out the door.

She was smiling to herself, as if she was a little kinky and might say or do anything.

"You live on the campus?" said Moss.

"Uh-huh. The Union. Three hundred women and *no men*. You?" Her hair hung loose and long over the collar of her coat.

"I have a room in the back of a house."

She stared into his eyes as though she was trying to read something on the back of his head. And all at once, Moss started getting hot, and flustered, and nervous. Students entering and leaving the bookstore were forced to walk around them as they stood in breathy silence. He glanced about quickly, saw no one who knew him, and spoke bluntly.

"Want to go there?"

"Sure."

"I mean right now."

"Okay." And he walked her nervously to his car.

Her name, she said, was Aranel. She was a drama major, was going to be a great Broadway star, and had picked him up because he was the only one in the bookstore who didn't look like a kid.

"Sometimes I get so horny I pick up my purse and throw it at the wall. My roommates think I'm nuts."

Moss veered off the road but straightened out in time to avoid a bicyclist. He parked at the entrance to his landlord's driveway, and they walked past the wide-porched, tree-shaded house, Moss trying to spot observers behind the window screens while the girl talked on at stage volume about Thoreau and trees.

He opened the door to his room and helped her off with her coat. Her clothes and body were full and matronly, rather than girlish. She was built like somebody's aunt.

Moss's bed, desk, and chair left barely enough space in the room to walk. But the afternoon sun was streaming in the shadeless window, and there wasn't a thing to drink.

"Would you like to dance?"

"Sure."

He turned on his squawky table-model radio, and they began moving clumsily back and forth, bumping the bed, the chair, then the desk. Moss kissed her cheek, then her neck, then full on the mouth. When they came up for air, the radio was into the news. They bumped against the chair, then sat down on the bed, and Moss began fumbling at her clothes.

"Easy. Easy."

"I can't wait."

She was like an artichoke, with layers and layers of clothing. And each layer was a different, gaudier color. Drab, brownish dress; peach slip; mint-green panties.

"Don't take off my glasses. I'm blind without them."

And the glasses stayed on through an afternoon's and evening's gymnastics in the hot, cramped room. They were clumsy together: Moss clipped her jaw with his elbow, she kneed him between the legs, they slid off the mattress and got wedged in the narrow space between the wall and the bed. No matter. Their own recklessness excited them further, drove them on. In between, they stared at one another with astonishment.

"What's it like for you?" Moss asked.

"At first it hurts, but then it feels like heaven."

About nine o'clock, Moss and the girl tiptoed past the darkened porch, and he drove her to a drive-in restaurant for a hamburger. Afterwards, at her request, he dropped her at the History Department.

"When will I see you again?"

"Call me." And she hurried away down a long line of sandstone columns.

Moss, sapped, sat back happily against the car's tattered upholstery. Who says reading doesn't get you places?

The next afternoon, he called the number she had given him and got an exterminator. The Union had no resident by her name. And though he took long, close looks at almost every girl he saw in the library, in class, and at the bookstore, Moss couldn't find her. The only thing he remembered about her for sure was her butter-fly-frame glasses. He decided she'd either bought new ones or dropped out of school.

The month of January was a rain-out. It poured almost every day, and even on the days it didn't rain, the streets were so puddled the pavement looked as if it would turn to mud. Moss caught a cold and felt that he was melting inside. And a young girl he tried to speak with on the campus addressed him as "sir." He took to his room and kept to himself.

Moss had entered college at twenty-five, a determined man. He was determined to get out of working in the brewery and stay out. Since leaving the Army, he'd worked on a bottling line, doing exactly the same work over and over again until it became as regular as breathing. Some nights he'd sit up in bed for hours, dreaming he was on the line and would be caught loafing. A college kid, working in the brewery for the summer, had pegged it.

"We're just appendages of a machine."

Moss wanted out, and college was the way.

All I know for certain is what I see. And what I see is this: Some men go off to work and come home filthy and tired. And others go off in white shirts and ties and they come home clean. I want to be one of the ones who come home clean.

He enrolled at a Catholic university in the middle of the city, took a straight liberal-arts major, hashed for his room and meals, and did well. Doctor Lanzavecchia, Professor of Political Science and his adviser, thought he should make politics his career.

"It's a fine vocation, not as highly regarded as it ought to be. Why, the President of the United States has the most important job in the world, next to the Pope."

"It's not for me," Moss said.

They strolled one evening across the campus, which was mostly a parking lot, Moss towering over the balding, mustached professor. Lanzavecchia's right shoulder had a permanent droop from years of carrying his heavy brief case.

"Well, study law, medicine, *something*. Don't just get out of school and be a salesman. Get yourself into a *profession*."

Some men, it seemed, came home cleaner than others.

"And don't go to a state university for your graduate work. You'll lose your faith."

Doctor Lanzavecchia climbed into his red sports car; he started the engine and idled it noisily for twenty seconds by his watch. Then he blessed himself and roared off, leaving Moss in a mist of burned rubber and exhaust fumes.

Moss had decided to become a lawyer.

When he tired of waiting for the orchard ground to dry, Moss dug out his G.I. boots and slogged among the trees in a light rain. Mud sucked at his feet and wind shook the trees; branches had been blown down and at least one tree had fallen. Fresh tracks were clustered around the bigger puddles; little many-toed prints marked where a raccoon had crouched to wash his food. There was always something to see, always a new discovery. A man could spend a lifetime getting to know just one orchard.

Law school had brought Moss out of the city and into another variety of life; and he fell for the drab, routine ways of a rural community as only a boy raised in the city can. He was a lover, blind to faults; an explorer; a discoverer. He was young enough to expect to make a living doing something he liked.

Moss had imagined his future only in the vaguest terms: comfort interrupted by kicks. Now, alone at his desk, looking out the window at the rain, he examined his own wants and needs.

If I opened a law office in a small town, I'd be my own man right from the start. An expert on property, estates, and riparian rights. And after a while, when I got to know the people and the territory, I'd watch for foreclosures or estate sales and pick up a small orchard of my own. Then I'd have a place to go and be alone and walk and work.

No big sprawling ranch house. No big silent car. What do I really need beyond a suit that isn't stained and a car that starts without a shove?

II

The grim weather continued, and so did Moss's purposeful mood. Through the Dean's office, he was given the name of a lawyer in a small valley town that owed its existence to grapes and peaches. Moss wrote the man, asking for advice, and the lawyer wrote back, suggesting Moss come and see him.

On a wet weekend when it was almost spring, Moss headed inland, his car's windshield wipers dragging and its doors tied shut with clothes rope. He rolled into town like some Dust Bowl migrant thirty years late, parked his heap around the corner from the county courthouse, hopped out, and stumbled against the high small-town curb. An old woman, hunched like a question mark, inching her way out of a used-appliance store, almost keeled over when she saw him, in a kind of sympathetic vibration. As Moss got up, she steadied herself.

"Y-you t-tore your p-p-pants." She smiled crookedly and started shuffling away.

Moss brushed himself off irritably and headed into the courthouse, a thick, old, gloomy building made of stone, with thirty-foot ceilings and veined marble walls. In a corner of the foyer, another old woman worked a switchboard in a cashier's cage by the light of a gooseneck lamp.

"Is Mister Pasquinelli here?"

She thumbed hurriedly through a stack of messages.

17

"Yes, yes." Then, pleased that she'd found it, "He's in Judge Malatesta's chambers, second floor."

Moss rode up in a rickety birdcage elevator and got off in a tall corridor where voices leaked through the transoms, droning lawyers' tones and hesitant testimony. At Judge Malatesta's door, he knocked.

"Come in!"

The anteroom was empty, but he heard people talking in Italian and laughter from the inner office. A short, thick, swarthy man, dressed elegantly in a blue suit with vest, leaned out of the judge's office.

"Mister Moss?" he said softly. "Come in." And he put his hand at Moss's back and guided him inside. A bald man, whose long-nosed, full-lipped face resembled the first man's, sat at a large, cluttered desk listening wearily to a fat young man with rosy cheeks and hair that spilled over his head like black ink. They all had the same short, chunky build and long noses and resembled one another like a family of bears.

"Paul," said the man in the vest, and the Italian conversation stopped, "this is Raymond Moss, who is studying law. Raymond, my cousin, Judge Paul Malatesta; and my nephew, Frank Silvera; I'm Vincent Pasquinelli."

His hands beckoned everyone to meet; they swooped and dived like birds. The nephew, who was younger than Moss, eyed him narrowly as they shook hands.

"You write a good letter," said Pasquinelli, full lips and a trim gray mustache smiling. "That's good for a lawyer."

"Thank you." Moss pressed his legs together to cover the rip in his trousers. "I hope to practice here someday."

Judge Malatesta said something to Pasquinelli in

Italian, and they both laughed. The young, plump man blushed and scowled.

"Come on," said Pasquinelli, gently pushing Moss toward the door, "I'll show you around. Paul, Frank, we'll meet you for lunch."

The lawyer's bulky elegance was a startling contrast to the drab courthouse halls and the dowdy people who lounged about them. Kids in denim jackets waiting to pay traffic fines, weathered old men talking in Italian and smoking black cigars, rich litigants in new overalls, poorer farmers in older ones. Most of them knew Pasquinelli and greeted him.

"Buon giorno."

The ones who didn't know him seemed to wish they did. The two men toured the jail, saw police court, and listened for a while to a lawsuit. The bailiffs, the cops, even the idlers on the steps outside, had friendly words for the lawyer.

Promptly at noon, Pasquinelli took Moss to a Victorian mansion, a two-block walk from the courthouse, that had been made over into a restaurant. Moss was growing accustomed to the lawyer's hand gently touching his shoulder, plucking at his elbow, or describing the people in a group like a painter's hand without a brush.

An indulgent maître d' moved them into the dining room past a long line of waiting cusomers and to a large corner table, where the judge and the nephew sat, arguing. The boy was a lawyer of some kind, too. Eager to prove himself, he took issue with everything his two older relatives said in both English and Italian. They went at it hotly until the waiter came.

Wearied again by the clash, the judge sat back and let his cousin place his order. Then he turned to Moss.

"You want to practice law here? What's the matter with your home?"

"Nothing," said Moss, caught short by the direct question. "I just like the country."

"You have people here? Relatives?"

"No."

"But you expect people to trust you with their money and their personal affairs."

Moss found himself being courteously sheepish. "Well, I'm not set exactly on this town—I mean city— just one like it. Maybe."

The judge eyed him, then sat back and seemed to drift off.

"We've just taken on Frank here." Pasquinelli, growling through a mouthful of salad, nodded to the boy, who frowned and blushed again. "And he's our first new man in six years."

Moss began to squirm. He felt a draft up his pants leg.

"I wouldn't work for somebody else. I'd open my own office."

Pasquinelli nodded. "Who was the last man to start a practice here, Paul? Mendoza? He handles Mexicans mostly. Drunk and disorderly. Traffic cases. Nickels and dimes."

"There was the fella on K Street," the judge said; "what was his name?"

"Couldn't make a go of it," said Pasquinelli. "And he was an Armenian."

"Pass the bread," said the boy.

The table, the town, and the countryside were slipping away. Moss wished he could leave.

"We're losing people here," Pasquinelli continued. "Population count went down in the last census."

"Hasn't even been a new doctor in town since the war," the judge said with a smug finality.

Moss turned on him. "Then you'd better get some younger people."

The judge, not prepared to be nasty, backed off. "You're right." He nodded his shiny dome. "You're absolutely right. Too many good young people running off to the city. But to come into a place where you don't know a soul—what do you think, Vincent?"

Pasquinelli shook his head. "I wouldn't advise it, but then I'm not your age. You have to start with a fair chance, remember. A place this size—why, everybody knows everybody else. And when someone gets in trouble, he looks for a friend, not just a lawyer. Ability, cleverness—those things mean a lot more in a big city. Lots of opportunity there."

"Here, too," cautioned the judge, wagging a finger, "here, too."

"Right," continued Pasquinelli. "We've got a promising future here, new industry coming in. But it's not here yet."

The judge and Pasquinelli, warming to the subject, began to talk about the businesses and factories the Chamber of Commerce, of which they both were members, would be luring into the area. The nephew listened, chewing. Moss finished his lunch in silence.

Afterwards, Pasquinelli walked him back toward the courthouse. Wonderful city. Great place to raise a family. Hope you decide to settle here. But.

"Give you a lift anywhere?" He stopped beside his car, a large black Lincoln.

"No thanks," said Moss. "I'm parked around the corner."

"Well, good luck then. Let me hear from you. And say hello to Doctor Fogdall."

"I'll do that." Moss had never heard of the man.

The lawyer drove away, and Moss walked dejectedly back to his own car. It had a parking ticket.

As he headed home, splashing through the valley towns in a light rain, he noticed a certain likeness between the town he'd visited and the ones he passed. It wasn't just the ugly civic offices, the sprawling food-processing plants or the newer drive-in restaurants and motels, wrong from the start, like babies with birth defects. After all, those are only buildings. In each town, a name appeared over a gas station, then turned up again on a market, and reappeared again outside a real-estate office. In one town it was Italian, in another Spanish, in a third Greek. But in every community one name, one family was predominant. And families outlast buildings.

Grow up in a town and you own it. Grow up in a city and it owns you.

Moss had to buy his independence. And there was no Moss winery, no Moss packing plant. He owned nothing negotiable.

He drove through the dark, an edgy stranger in each neon town, relaxing only in the miles of black farmland between. At the last liquor store before the campus, he bought a pint of bourbon and took it home. He drank only part of it, sank heavily onto his bed, and fell asleep quickly in the overheated room.

Every man needs a dream to lean on. When he loses one, he must find another. And Moss, whose idea of a small-town law practice had been as vivid and as temporary as a county fair, began the search again.

He would be a farmer, leave school and find simple

work out in the country, save his money and buy his own place. He began reading agricultural magazines, dull periodicals with pictures of outsize steers or ears of corn on the covers. One authoritative journal offered, in its spring issue, a complete breakdown of the economics of small farming. Moss sat down hungrily at a library table to read it.

The statistics turned out to be downright discouraging, and those for fruitgrowers worst of all. According to government figures, it took an investment of a hundred thousand dollars in a fruit ranch to return an income of five thousand dollars a year. Yet wages were so low, they were all the way out of the nation's economic reality, and fruit pickers had to be imported from Mexico. That ruled out Moss's future thoughts of working his way up, and his existing plans for a summer job. The way things added up, the fruit-growing business, like small-town law, could be entered only by way of the womb.

Moss brooded for weeks and thought about re-enlisting in the Army. He could qualify for a commission.

And then everything seemed to break, starting with the weather. One morning it was summer. Just like that. Clear, hot, blue and white, warm enough to swim in the water that had fallen the week before. Moss put away his raincoat for another year. And the girls started wearing cottons and began to tan.

In a week, the orchard went white with blossoms. Each branch burst into puff-popcorn flowers in a change as elemental and precise as a calm sea turning choppy. The orchard floor was thick with shadow and a fragrance too perfumey to be real. The ground was still damp, but the sun was hot enough to make you dizzy.

Moss sunned himself, and stretched, and walked up a sweat, and watched the buds and blossoms. Standing in the trees, all by himself, he smiled.

That same week, through the secretary to the Dean of the Law School, he received a letter from Pasquinelli.

The lawyer recounted Moss's visit to his community and his interest in the town's future. An acquaintance of Pasquinelli, a builder named O'Malley, had opened the first contemporary real-estate development in their area. These new houses represented a large increase in the number of available dwellings, and there were some fears that the community was now overbuilt. To protect the investment, O'Malley was planning to staff up with sales personnel during the summer. He needed energetic young men with poise and brains, and—lets face it—the town was short of these to start with. It was an excellent chance for a young man not only to earn good money (salary plus commission) but it was a fine opportunity for the *right* young man to establish himself in the area as well. Would Moss be interested? He wrote the lawyer that he would and could report for work any time after the middle of June.

The flowers fell a petal at a time and littered the earth like confetti. Leaves, green and glossy in the sunshine, took their place. Moss boned for his year-end examinations in their shade, and for all his wandering and dozing, fared better than he would have if he'd shut himself in his room. He packed and left after his last exam, without even waiting long enough to pick up his final grades.

The countryside was already turning brown, and only the tilled fields along the valley floor remained green. But in these enormous rectangles, the low vegetable plants and the fruit-and-nut-growing trees sprang from the black ground with a jungle-like intensity, as though they'd sucked minerals and moisture from the pale, distant hills. Even the town looked healthier in the sunshine. Women and girls paraded the streets in bare-armed summer frocks, the men wore Panama hats, and the ugly old courthouse cast a cool and noble shadow.

Moss stopped first at Pasquinelli's office, and the lawyer seemed genuinely glad to see him. Together, they rode out of town in Moss's car to meet O'Malley.

The development was spread over gently rolling acreage that had formerly been a pig farm, and something of the old atmosphere remained. The valley sun beat down pitlessly and baked a foul stench out of the earth. And around the foundations, the houses were splashed with ugly mud. Though they appeared large at a distance, they were actually rather small and of such flimsy stucco construction it looked as if you could kick holes right through the walls. It was the exterior colors —green, violet, pink—that made them seem larger than they actually were.

There was no landscaping of any kind. In fact, there didn't seem to be a tree from the highway to the horizon.

On the new black streets there were no other cars, moving or parked. Nor were there any carpenters at work on the unfinished frames on every block. A hot, oppressive torpor seemed to have worn everything to a halt.

When Moss's car pulled up at the tract office—a ranch-style house with a sign staked out in front—a strange-looking man in a green blazer ran eagerly outside to greet what he evidently thought were prospects. From the waist up he had the proportions of a tall man

——long trunk, thin dangling arms, long neck. But below the waist his legs were short and thick, and he had an enormous paunch. He could have been put together in Mexico. His face was red and meaty, and his black hair was fast disappearing.

"Here comes O'Malley," said the lawyer.

When he recognized Pasquinelli, the disappointed builder slowed his step. He looked sad-faced and moist-eyed, a salesman hoping for the best even when he knows the best is going to be pretty awful. In a desperate grasp at a cheerful opener, he pounded his fist on the sprung hood of Moss's car.

"A *Frazer!* For Chrissake, I didn't know they made 'em any more."

Pasquinelli maintained his reserve. "Gerry, this is Ray Moss, who I told you about."

"Hiya, Ray. Buddy a mine had one a these. Says to this day it was the best car he ever owned. Wouldn't be interested in selling it, would you?"

"This? Hell, yes."

But the offer was withdrawn as soon as he'd accepted. "Solid. Look at that top—rolled it, did you?"

"The last owner did. She went off a highway and turned over in a ditch, but she wasn't hurt."

"Isn't that something? Don't make 'em like they used to, do they?"

The car door let out a groan as the builder opened it. On a wave of his conversation, they rode inside the office, O'Malley talking like a drowning man who hoped buoyant words would keep him afloat.

"How's business?" the lawyer interrupted.

"Picking up," O'Malley answered automatically. "Had an elderly couple looking yesterday, nice folks, who said these are the best homes they've seen for the price in this part of the state. And they've been looking for *months*."

The builder was sweating heavily, and he smelled of mouthwash as though it were coming out of his pores. Ignoring Moss, he talked to Pasquinelli, praising the houses, the prospects, and the lawyer himself in terms so fawning and abject as to be downright embarrassing. It was clear he worked for Pasquinelli.

"It's going to pick up, Mr. Pasquinelli. I just *know* it is." There was a whining tone in his voice that made Moss turn away and look out a window. Pasquinelli finally muttered something harsh to O'Malley, which silenced him. Pasquinelli seemed to take charge after that and ushered Moss outside for a tour of the development.

"Good man, O'Malley," Pasquinelli said as they walked up an empty street. "People have been criticizing him all too unfairly, if you ask me."

Moss said nothing, but looking back over his shoulder, he saw the builder staring forlornly after them.

"What did you think of him?"

"He seemed very friendly," said Moss lamely.

"I *thought* you'd notice that. He's that way with everybody. It's his *gift*, don't you see? He's a great salesman!"

"I'll bet he is."

"Of course! I don't know where we'd be without him." Pasquinelli seemed to be arguing with himself.

They turned a corner and walked down a spotless white sidewalk that reflected sunlight so bright it made them squint.

"They're not bad houses," Pasquinelli said, "when you consider what good ones cost these days."

They came abruptly to the end of the street, which

halted as if driven back by a dense growth of brush and weeds.

"Local people have invested a good deal of money in this development, Raymond—myself included. It's important that these homes *sell*. If you came to work here, and worked very hard, and were willing to advance yourself, there's no telling how far you could go. Or how fast. Do you understand me?"

"I think so." Moss was also beginning to understand what gave O'Malley his hunted look. His job was open to whoever could take it. He had no equity.

"Isn't there a state examination for real-estate salesmen?" Moss asked.

"You let me worry about that," said Pasquinelli. "O'Malley will conclude the deals and sign all the necessary papers. But you'll get a full commission on every sale you make. We watch the sales very closely, and we'll know who's responsible for any increase."

They walked along the hot white sidewalk toward the office, but instead of going inside, Pasquinelli asked Moss to drive him back to town. They left without saying good-bye to O'Malley, and Moss could feel the man looking after them again from inside.

Pasquinelli had reserved a room in an old house that reminded Moss of a decaying Southern mansion, complete with huge magnolia tree out front. In the dark lobby, a row of lonely elders sat waiting for god knows what, watching the world go by outside a window.

Moss's room was on the second floor, about halfway along a hallway where old women continually shuffled past in bathrobes. His room had heavy carved furniture including a chest of drawers that would crush a man if it ever fell on him. His bed was a sagging mattress in a large brass frame, and a green sports coat that matched

O'Malley's was hanging in the closet. After dark the musty hallways echoed with desperate hacking coughs.

In the morning a thick ground fog was smothering the town. Wearing his green blazer, which was a size too small, Moss drove slowly out of town, headlights ablaze, creeping along the highway in the right-hand lane. When he came to the tract turnoff, he stopped.

If I keep going, I'll be in the city by noon. Through with this town and these crummy houses. And tomorrow? I'd be back at work in the brewery.

He spun the wheel and drove among the boxy houses until he found the one with the sign out front. O'Malley was nowhere in sight, and the office was locked. There seemed to be no one else around. Moss walked out back of the nearest house and looked in through the windows.

The houses were only stucco, it is true, but that's solid-enough construction for a climate without snow. And the rooms were a fairly good size, although the bedrooms could be larger. There just seemed to be something missing in these particular houses, even when compared with the modest ones in town.

O'Malley showed up a little after ten, waddling up the walk to open the office with a key on a long gold chain. His eyes were red and bleary, and he smelled of booze beneath his mouthwash; he still managed to exude a kind of queasy optimism.

"Sorry I'm late. Not much doing here anyway, was there? It'll pick up this afternoon."

Shakily, the builder set a pot of coffee perking on an electric hot plate.

"I thought I'd take a look at the model home first . . ." Moss began.

"Aw, sit down. There's lots of time for that."

O'Malley unbuttoned his coat and put his feet up on a desk that was both battered and new. "You follow football?"

Moss offered a few opinions about the university's team, but law school had kept him out of touch. O'Malley filled in the rest. He knew more about Moss's school than Moss did, and soon he was re-creating great games out of the past like a sportscaster, with scores, names, and play by play.

"Army-Notre Dame in forty-seven," said Moss; "there was a great one."

"The Black Knights of the Hudson versus the Fighting Irish with number one national ranking at stake." O'Malley filled a cup to the brim with black coffee and handed it to Moss, who put his feet up on the builder's cluttered desk. He poured another for himself.

"Blanchard and Davis versus Lujack in the Battle of the Century. Yankee Stadium, New York, filled to capacity."

Man by man, O'Malley announced the starting line-ups, cupping his hands to sound like a public-address system. "At left tackle: Number 80, George Connor. Left half: Emil 'Six-Yard' Sitko. Quarterback for Army: Arnold Tucker."

O'Malley could even make crowd noise. Leaping to his feet, he continued. "Third quarter, no score. Blanchard breaks free. He's in the open. Forty. Thirty. One man between the Doc and the goal line. It's the Polack, playing safety. Wham! They collide—the Doc goes down. Final score: Notre Dame, nothing; Army, nothing."

O'Malley began to sing. "On, dear old Army team, on to the fray . . . ON YOUR FEET, LAD . . ."

And Moss got up and joined him, waving his coffee cup like a beer stein. They swung into "Cheer, cheer for old Notre Dame."

And suddenly Moss was there, in the stands with a loud-mouthed Irishman, swigging on a flask and singing, seeing it all—bands, color, contact, dizzy from excitement, hoarse from cheering.

They coughed with laughter until the tears flowed.

"Oh Christ, boy," said O'Malley, "whatever are you doing in this godforsaken place with a broken-down old Mick like me?"

"I dunno."

"It's a terrible place. If pricks were wings, this town would be an air force."

The fact that O'Malley spoke in seriousness convulsed Moss once again.

"You're all right, Ray—that's your name, isn't it? You're all right. Oh, by Jesus." O'Malley looked at a watch almost hidden on his hairy wrist. "It's noon. Let's go eat."

"Shall I lock up?"

"Hell, no. Nothing here worth taking."

They walked out to Moss's car, and finding the door on his side tied shut, O'Malley climbed clumsily through the window and collapsed on the seat. "Ahhhrrrr. Through the window in silent stealth like a cat burglar."

They cruised out onto the highway and headed another mile or so out beyond the town to a large chicken-and-hamburger shack where several trucks were parked.

"Here it is, boy. Tough food but tender waitresses. And all they ever get a chance to talk to is teamsters."

They entered noisily, O'Malley greeting the girls inside with an enthusiasm that was not returned. A young, black-haired girl with skin like fresh milk approached them shyly.

"Good morning. We have hamburgers, cheeseburgers, or fried chicken."

O'Malley bent over and checked out her legs. "You got a nice pair of rails, honey. I'd like to follow 'em to the station."

She stared at him, openly bewildered. "You sure have a funny way of talking."

"Ah, you perk up a man's appetite, my dear, and arouse all sorts of carnal desires."

"Would you like some coffee?"

"I'll have a hamburger," Moss interrupted.

"Make that two, me little lily of the valley," O'Malley added. "You're new here, aren't you?"

"I just got out of school."

"Well, you're a nice girl, and pretty, too."

She blushed and smiled and walked away with the order, about six inches off the ground.

After lunch O'Malley picked up his sports narrative exactly where he'd left off. He really had an easy way of talking when he wasn't trying to impress anybody. Gradually, he drew Moss out. They talked baseball and swapped Army stories, and by midafternoon, when the first prospects of the day turned up, the two of them were all wound up from talking and laughing.

A young couple, pushing a baby in a stroller, moved along the sidewalk. They were bashful browsers, speaking quietly and exchanging understanding glances. When O'Malley burst out of the office, the woman jumped.

"Hello there! Have you come to look at a house?"

"No," the man answered, backing off, "we're just out for a walk."

"Then come on in and have some coffee, for Chrissake! And bring the little fella."

They looked at each other, then did just as O'Malley said. The husband, it turned out over coffee, had been a swimmer on the local high-school team, and he and O'Malley assessed United States prospects in the next Olympic Games. Moss, opening up himself, made faces at the baby and talked to the mother about the techniques of child care.

When O'Malley at last brought up the subject of the house, it was as a normal part of the conversation, just as a man offers a visitor a tour of his own home. The couple were struck the same way, of course, and gladly let the man show them bedrooms, bathrooms, family room, and garage. They politely complimented O'Malley on everything, and he just as politely thanked them. And when he mentioned the price of the house, it was as if a close friend was offering them a chance to get in early on a fantastic deal. In fact, it sounded so good they signed an Agreement of Sale form and left a check with O'Malley as a deposit on a house. The builder even seemed a little reluctant to part with the property.

"We'll take good care of the place, Mr. O'Malley," the mother said earnestly.

"It's a pleasure to have you in the neighborhood," the builder assured them as they left.

"Jesus," said Moss with respect in his voice, "you made it look easy."

"Do you know something, lad?" O'Malley confessed as he waved them a good-bye. "I almost forgot to show them the house at all."

It was, he said, the first sale he'd made in over

a month. And when it was time to close up for the day, he seemed to cloud over with a kind of trouble all his own.

"It's been a good day. I don't remember when I had so much fun in the daytime and sober."

He had indeed made it look easier than it really was. They sold no more houses that week. But the days passed pleasantly. O'Malley and Moss walked all over the tract and through the houses where work had halted in different phases of construction. They decided which teams were likely to meet in the World Series, agreed that Oriental women were the most desirable type, and picked an all-time all-America football team. There was plenty of time to reflect and daydream.

And then, about two o'clock on Sunday afternoon, they were invaded. Suddenly, carloads of people began arriving. They moved slowly along the streets—parents, children, and old folks inside, gaping out at the houses.

O'Malley watched as the flash flood of traffic swept over his street, some cars dropping out of line to park while whole families emptied out of them. "Here they come," he said without surprise, "the burpers. All filled up with Sunday dinner and looking for something to do. They come out here and walk all over everything, ask you silly questions, and belch. Most of them have no intention at all of buying a house."

"What do we do?" asked Moss.

"Show 'em around, what else?" O'Malley answered. And he stepped outside to smile a greeting at the first family coming up the walk.

The people seemed to be of all ages, all incomes. They drove new cars; they drove old ones. They were dressed for church; they wore sloppy sports clothes. The kids ran through the houses and skipped along the sidewalk. The women tended to examine the furnishings in the model homes more closely than the homes themselves. And the men looked as though they would rather not be there at all. The people who seemed most interested, who stayed a long while and asked a lot of questions and talked as though they were genuinely knowledgeable about the building business (much more so than Moss, to his embarrassment), invariably turned out to be not interested at all. They had simply done more shopping. O'Malley had them pegged, all right. Even to the belching. They kept coming until dark, and it didn't get dark until after eight o'clock.

"I suppose I should have warned you," the builder said when the streets were at last empty again, "but there's no way to spot the ones who aren't buying. About all you can do is avoid getting cornered. I ask them a direct question—what's your name or what's your phone number—and if they start weaseling, I get rid of them. Anyway, I think we got a couple of good leads out of it, and it doesn't look like they swiped anything."

The next day everything was back to sleepy normality, and Moss and O'Malley enjoyed a very poor business day.

Now that he had help, O'Malley could begin canvassing the area for prospects. He had Moss start tracking people down with a newspaper and a telephone. "First you turn to the page where they list the births, see? All the names and addresses. Each of those is a family that's just grown by one. Call on all of 'em, and maybe you find somebody who'll come out and look at a house. Or here, in the deaths—families of people who died. Here where it says beloved father of so on and so forth. Well, the so on and so forth are about to come into a little money, or think they are, which is the same thing. So you call on all of them. Then, of course, there's the weddings and even the divorces. It's the whole circle of life, lad. You throw it out like a big lasso, and when you haul it in, you've roped a few prospects."

While Moss threw out the big lasso, O'Malley went fishing. He made personal calls on all the people he'd had a line on earlier and hadn't had time to get in touch with. They worked at it all the next week, Moss roping and O'Malley feeling for nibbles; and on Sunday, when the burpers returned, there were some buyers among them.

They sold a house and then another. And the next week there were coveralled moving men unloading furniture on the sidewalk.

When Moss had learned how to determine who was genuinely interested in a house and who was not, he and O'Malley worked out a system. Moss would take customers on a tour of at least two houses, following O'Malley's instructions: "Show 'em a lemon and then sell against it. And don't stop talking." If they were burpers, he got rid of them immediately afterwards. But if the parties seemed interested and solvent, he brought them back to the office, where O'Malley waited to close the deals. While he talked, Moss listened outside the door; and when he heard O'Malley bullying and wheedling the customers in a quiet, intense voice, he felt the same digusted feeling he'd had when the builder had talked with Pasquinelli. Moss tried to ignore the ugly talk, the pressure, the threats. But it was often the ugliest talk that sold a house. And O'Malley seemed to thrive on it. Flushed with success, he seemed almost healthy.

"Does it have to be like that?" Moss asked him after he'd badgered a man with five kids into buying a three-bedroom home.

"That's the job," said the builder, running a comb through his greasy hair. He'd made it a challenge.

Now when people came out to the development, they began to see signs of human occupancy: wash hanging on a line, children playing in the streets. Most people found this reassuring.

The ones who had already moved in brought their friends out to testify to the wisdom of their choice. And some of the friends began to think about moving. Slowly Moss and O'Malley were getting under way. A change had happened, a change in attitude like a change in season. Something no one had really wanted very much was becoming desirable.

When they'd made their fourth sale, O'Malley ordered the contractor back to work, and soon carpenters were hammering and sawing in the dormant frames. A roofer's truck gave off the stench of boiling tar.

The two men's promoting had at first been mostly a means of passing time. Now the prospects they had hunted began to devour what time they had left. They were busy every day and most nights. On the weekends they drove themselves hardest, to handle the extra crowds. Some evenings Moss had a kind of kink in his face from smiling. On the job he and O'Malley chatted only in passing. They ate lunch in shifts, and there was suddenly no time for gab any more.

Moss was making money. More of it, and faster, than he ever had before. He soon had enough for a new suit, and then enough for a good car. He didn't buy these things right away, but just knowing that he could gave him a kind of independence he had never known before.

O'Malley took on extra help: Russ, an older man with a limp who'd had a small real-estate business of his own, and a delicate youngster named Buddy who'd dropped out of the county junior college. He walked from the ankles down, his arms stiff at his sides, gliding along as if his feet were wheels. There were more green blazers on the streets, but more prospects, too. It didn't get any easier.

After a full day of greeting strangers and talking to them and leading them to O'Malley, or slipping them his business card, Moss couldn't unwind. He'd leave work, stop off for a quick meal on the way into town, and then sit in his room, reviewing a list of people who had promised to call back. Later, sweaty, sore-footed, and tight-jawed, he'd collapse on his mushy mattress, only to find he was too tied up to sleep.

The job, he noticed with some satisfaction, was getting to O'Malley, too. From his looks, he was drinking more. And Moss could feel himself being watched. It was time to get away for a while. He told O'Malley he'd like to take a couple of days off and go out of town.

O'Malley, with a tired, commiserating smile, agreed. "Where is it you plan to go?"

"Back to school, just to look around."

"Well, that sounds exciting. Look out for them co-eds. One of 'em might try to put the make on you."

Moss took the remark sullenly. Things had got that bad.

Early the next morning he gassed up his car and headed out of the flat, cultivated countryside. The miles of fields had come to seem empty and mechanical, like an outdoor factory. By comparison, the town had grown small. It seemed that the farmland, surrounding the town and already quivering in the morning heat, could swallow it without showing a bulge.

An orchard doesn't seem like much when orchard's all there is.

Soon hills swelled up out of the flatlands, and dark brown mountains with patches of green pushed the road into loops and bends. The air was light, and Moss could breathe without feeling he was being inflated.

Just before noon he checked into a pink motel near the university's campus. He changed immediately into his old easy-fitting hickory shirt and khakis and went wandering. The orchard seemed to be as he remembered it. Controlled and parklike, in clear contrast to the busy highway. The trees cut off the direct sun like long lines of parasols. Everything was light above them, everything dark below. The trees looked shaggy, wilted, slightly faded. The outer leaves, at the top and around the periphery of the branches, were bleached a pale yellow. Even the air was cool within their shade, and as Moss walked, he scuffed up little puffs of dust along the orchard floor.

He walked parallel to the highway, passing through the ranks of trees like an inspecting general. And at about where he estimated the center of the orchard to be, he sat down and leaned against a trunk. A silence began in that place, a shaft of unbroken quiet that reached upward to the stars.

He sank into sleep like a stone and sprawled on the ground at the foot of the tree. Earth got into his mouth and ears and clogged his wide nostrils, affecting him like a drug. He slept so deep that he had a dream, and even in that dream he was asleep.

Perhaps he would have rested there for years, a

plum-orchard Rip van Winkle with a long white beard, had a faint and foreign sound not pierced his peace.

It was an even mechanical noise, an engine sound that instead of pulling its load away and passing on, like a truck or bus, remained. Moss stirred and then sat up, bewildered. He tasted dirt. A speck was in his eye. And there was a machine where a machine hadn't been before. He got up and walked in the direction of the sound.

It grew louder as he came numbly through the trees, echoing unseen like a shout in a forest. It strained and then relaxed. And then strained again. Suddenly Moss came to the end of the trees, where trees had grown before. Now the orchard stopped abruptly at a row of little stakes with ribbon tied around them. Beyond, raw earth stretched to the nearest hill, crisscrossed by deep tire tracks and the hard square marks of metal treads. A yellow tractor, rumbling and creaking, pushed a steel blade over the ground, skimming off the cover. When it came to a tree, the driver stopped and backed off a little, then took a running shove at the trunk, the engine laboring against the stubborn object until the branches went down in the dirt and the roots were pried up. Then the tree was shoved aside into a gully full of trees, most still fresh and green. Some bore ripening fruit.

Moss stood behind the ribbon stakes and stared, dirty-faced and open-mouthed, as the trees fell and were shoved aside as so much useless debris.

A man wearing a metal hat and carrying a clipboard kept an eye on the tractor from the shade of one of the remaining trees. The tractor operator watched the levers, tracks, and blade of his machine expressionlessly. He seemed to be shoving the dirt into a mound to make an access road leading from the highway. There, in a large area already cleared and flattened, other machinery, dump trucks and air compressors, waited like weapons marshaled for an invasion.

The tractor struck so swiftly and with such force, destroying in seconds what had taken years to cultivate, that the whole desolate lanscape held Moss in a dull fascination. At first he didn't hear the man in the hard hat yelling at him.

"Hey! Hey, you! Get outa there! You wanna get hurt?"

When he yelled loudly enough to be heard even over the tractor noise, Moss turned submissively and began the long, slow walk back through the trees. If was as if they were lined up, somber and silent, awaiting their own execution. The tractor racket echoed after him, louder, somehow, going back.

Moss blew the dirt out of his nose, brushed it out of his hair, picked it out of his ears.

Sooner or later, it's coming. Sooner or later, I am going to be left with nothing.

III

The next morning Moss returned, stood at the edge of the trees, and watched the bulldozer at work. He searched the faces of the two workmen for traces of guilt, like a churchman confronting a drunken sailor with a girl on his arm. But the men went about their systematic destruction with the bored preoccupation of employees doing any job, anywhere.

Moss derived no satisfaction from what he saw.

The plum orchard had not been touched. But all that stood between it and the tractor was a line of surveyor's stakes; a word was all it would take to cross over.

Before long the noisy indifference of the men and their machine drove Moss away. He plunged deeper into the trees than he ever had before and walked beyond the weathered shed where once he'd stopped to rest. Far back from the highway, he came upon a small, tidy white house with a carefully cultivated garden, like a witch's cottage in the woods. A tree loaded with grapefruit the size of bowling balls grew beside a bush of perfect red roses.

Off to one side of the house was a strange and gaudy structure, a homemade monument. It was a kind of tower about twenty feet high with an irregular broken shape like a pagoda. It had been pieced together with odd bric-a-brac, tile, statuary, rocks, spoke wheels, shells, flagstones, each item painted red, white, and blue. There were strange symbols, stars, the points of the compass, hex signs, painted on the supporting cement; and the whole structure tapered oddly to a pyramid point. A red-white-and-blue birdhouse was built into the cement about halfway. And there was a red-white-and-blue weather vane at the top. Parts of the structure were worn, the paint faded and cracked. The tower appeared to have been put together item by item over a long period of time; it represented years of work and looked like something you might see on top of the cake at a wedding of two people from Eastern Europe.

Before Moss could move in for a closer look, the front door of the house opened. Moss stepped back into the trees as a short, brown, lumpy man—like a baked potato with feet—shuffled out onto the porch. An old collie crept out of his way, and the man walked slowly around the front of the house. He looked sullen and unapproachable, and he muttered angrily to himself.

"Gnasheet!"

He disappeared around the back of the house, and shortly a violent metal-on-metal hammering started coming from the garage.

Moss turned back in the direction of the highway and walked away through the trees. For the first time he felt lucky that he hadn't been caught trespassing.

Even the college campus was torn by building workers. A new dormitory was under construction, and some older classrooms had been demolished. The main drive was torn up, and large cement links of sewer pipe were lined along the sidewalk. It was difficult to find a parking place.

Summer school was in session, but many of the classrooms were vacant. The campus walkways seemed sleepy without the groups of young students surging in and out of class. Now the students walked alone, or in pairs.

And they looked older. Teachers mostly, Moss guessed; there were even a couple of nuns.

That afternoon Moss sat alone on a stone bench that had been occupied all the rest of the school year and eavesdropped on an English lecture. When the bench began to feel hard, he got up and went into the library. The main reading room was emptier than Moss remembered it, but busier, too. Solitary students, deep in work, sat at the tables scribbling in notebooks or on three-by-five index cards. Some students were almost hidden behind piles of reference books; they might have been working there for days. They were quiet and remote, and there was none of the chatty visiting that was the rule during the normal school year.

Moss walked softly past the shelves, examining the books. Without the responsibility of study, a meal had become a feast. It was hard to decide where to begin. He settled for the Britannica as a starter and picked the volume that included "plums."

He pulled out a chair at one end of a long library table, empty except for a man wearing a green eyeshade, who sat piecing together pages of typescript with scissors and Scotch tape, near the opposite corner. Moss read briefly, without concentrating. And when he looked up, he saw the girl with the butterfly-frame glasses enter the room.

She carried an armload of books, which she set on the table next to Moss's. He stared, trying to catch her eye, but she sat down facing him in a businesslike manner and began reading, carefully underlining passages with a pencil and a ruler. Her hair was cut short, and she'd put on weight, but the glasses were unmistakable. Moss picked up his encyclopedia volume, carried it to the next table, and sat down directly opposite her. She glanced up and he smiled.

"Hi."

She looked at him blankly and then went back to her book. Moss fidgeted nervously with his.

"Aranel," he whispered, "I tried to call you back, but you gave me the wrong number."

She didn't look up.

"That's the truth. I swear it."

She gave him a polite smile. "I'm sorry, but you have the wrong person."

"Your name is Aranel," Moss insisted, and his voice rose out of a whisper.

"No, it isn't," she said patiently. And she turned back to her book.

Moss leaned back in his chair and chewed his fist. She did seem different. Calmer. Less outspoken. But it was the same girl. He leaned forward across the table again.

"We met at the bookstore last fall, remember?"

She made another polite smile, forcing it a little this time, and shook her head.

"We went up to my place."

"Please. Would you *mind*." She glared at him.

"We *slept* together."

It was out before he could stop himself. Moss glanced around the room. Nobody had heard; at least it looked that way. When he turned back, the girl's chin was trembling, and her eyes had gone moist.

"Look, I didn't mean to hurt you—it was your idea as much as mine."

She stared at him, wide-eyed and silent, and two large tears trickled out from behind her glasses and rolled down her cheeks.

"Please don't cry." Moss looked around. The student with the eyeshade was peering back at him. "I'll get you something. How about some coffee?" Moss set his book down and dashed around the table, bumping against the corner. "Come on, we'll go get some coffee."

She stood up, shakily willing, and he led her from the room, outside, and down the library steps. He fumbled for words. What do you say to a girl with brains?

"Aranel, maybe you forgot. But you ought to realize I *did* try to see you again. I called. I looked for weeks."

They ducked away from the small bugs that hung by strands from the trees along the path to the Student Union.

"My name is Barbara," she sniffled.

Moss blinked in surprise. Before the flustered girl could face forward again, she had walked directly into a tree.

"I'm all right; I'm *all right*," she insisted, near exasperation.

They walked along in silence then, while she regained an exaggerated calm. When they reached the cafeteria, Moss took her hand and led her to a table in a quiet corner. While he got the coffee, she dried her eyes with Kleenex.

"Feel better?" Moss asked with as much cheerfulness as he could muster.

She said nothing but took so big a sip she nearly gagged on it. She put her glasses back on, and they made her eyes alarmingly larger.

"That's how I remembered you—the glasses."

Her tranquillity made Moss uneasy. It seemed too much like fury suppressed.

"I dropped out of school last fall," she said in a drama

46

student's slightly oratorical voice. "I had a nervous breakdown. There were things that I said and did then that I don't remember, because I don't want to."

"I'm sorry," said Moss. Guilt clogged his throat. His coffee cooled, untouched.

"I just started back to school this summer. It's hard, getting used to the routine."

She brightened a little as she talked about herself, and Moss began to feel he'd done some good after all.

"Daddy didn't want me to come back here. For a while they thought I was pregnant."

Moss sank back again.

"It was a false alarm." The polite smile returned.

"Are you still studying drama?" Moss tried to divert the conversation.

"Oh, no. Psychology. I'm going into counseling. What about you?"

"I'm not in school this summer. I'm working down in the valley." He began to talk about the town, his job, the houses; but he stopped when he saw she wasn't listening. She seemed so relaxed, he thought she might fall asleep. So he offered to walk her back to the library. They stopped at the steps outside.

"Look, I have to go back tomorrow, and I'd like to see you tonight—if you're not doing anything."

She stared at him quizzically. "All right."

Moss pulled out the pencil he'd been holding in his pocket. And a business card. She gave him her address and telephone number.

"Sure it's the right one this time?"

But she didn't smile. He promised to call her at six o'clock and watched her walk up to the library steps. At the landing she turned and called to him.

"I'll put back your book," she said with a gaiety so sudden it took Moss completely by surprise. Then she disappeared into the dark doorway.

They went to a movie that evening, a highly regarded French film that turned out to be all embraces and subtitles; it was hard to keep track of both. Moss heard the girl sniffle softly in the dark at several parts of the picture. As they left, he put his arm around her, and she leaned against him. She laughed at his car when he untied the rope to open the door, and she snuggled up against him as he drove. He threaded his way through the campus and parked at the edge of a graveyard. She came to him eagerly, and they kissed. He touched her breasts and held her against him. When he began unbuttoning her blouse, she turned away and began to sob.

"No! No!"

"Oh, for Chrissake." Moss was about to explode with frustration. But that only made things worse. She shook with crying, a strange, measured "boo hoo hoo" like a character in a comic strip. He couldn't speak to her, much less touch her. Not until he'd backed his car out and started toward the campus did her sobbing subside. She looked out the window, keeping the back of her tousled hair toward Moss.

He didn't know what to say. All he could think of was "I'm sorry," but he wasn't. So they drove in silence.

Moss double-parked outside her dormitory. She sat staring through the window and then spoke in a small voice, violated and rejected, expecting disappointment.

"I don't suppose I'll see you again."

"Well, I don't get up this way very often."

The polite smile was back. "Thank you anyway for a very nice evening." She tried to open her door.

"Just a second—I'll untie it."

48

As he held the door open for her, she threw her arms around his neck and kissed him. And then hurried into the lobby. Moss stood stunned as she turned back the way she'd done at the library steps and called good night in a tearless, exhilarated voice that, he decided while driving back into the valley the following day, had been filled with pride.

Strange girl. She seemed to be fighting her instincts. She denied herself candy, dropped things, apologized. Her helplessness was overpowering. Stuck behind a truck and trailer, Moss rode sourly through the flat farmland and cooked valley air.

Some vacation.

His world was tearing, like a paper map. The orchard, his refuge, was under seige. The strange, lumpy man who lived there would surely be reached. The trees would be ripped out and a gas station or mortuary erected in their place. And nobody gave a good god damn about the waste. They don't make state parks out of orchards.

It would all be grabbed up, and there was nothing he could do about it. Passing the bar, making it as a lawyer, wouldn't get him the life he wanted. Because the orchard would be gone forever by the time he got the money to buy it. Unless he grabbed some of it himself.

And that set him to thinking about the plum orchard in a new and different way.

When Moss reported back to work in the morning, O'Malley wasn't there. According to Buddy, he hadn't been in for two days.

"It's just awful," Buddy said, wringing his hands nervously. "He keeps calling here, but he won't say where he is. And he sounds like he's been drinking."

Buddy and Russ, the older man, had done their best, but with Moss and O'Malley both gone, the work was too much for them to handle. The builder's desk was a mass of disorganized paper. They hadn't been able to find anything.

"He insulted Mister Pasquinelli," Buddy added. "Mister Pasquinelli's just *furious*."

Moss sat down and began sorting the papers, picking out anything that appeared urgent or seemed to need processing. Suppliers telephoned, looking for O'Malley. The contractor had to see him right away about something. Moss answered what questions he could, and stalled the other people off, while Buddy and Russ hustled prospects in and out of the houses.

About ten-thirty, O'Malley telephoned.

"Hello, Ray. How the hell are you?" A jukebox thumped and twanged in the background. O'Malley was coming through about ninety proof.

"Where *are* you?"

"Did you get any action up at that school?"

"No. Where *are* you?" Moss insisted.

"Fresno. Come on down and have a drink."

"Fresno? How did you get there?"

"Don't know. I just woke up the other morning and here I was. Will you join me, boy?"

His voice was wavy, but without regret. Moss grew annoyed.

"What's the idea, leaving the job like that . . ."

"What's the idea, my grandmother!" O'Malley shouted. "I quit, lad. Told Pasquinelli to go shit in his hat!"

"When?"

"Yesterday. On the phone. Never trust a man who ignores his impulses, boy."

"Look, tell me where you are, and I'll come and get you."

"Aw, you're all right, Ray. You know that?"

Moss heard O'Malley ask a bartender for the address. Then he passed it along.

"You're really coming down?"

"Yes. I'll leave right now."

"Oh, god love ya, boy." And with a clumsy clatter, he hung up the telephone.

It was a two-hour drive, and Moss grew angrier by the mile. The man had to be looked after like a child. No sense of responsibility. Complete lack of self-discipline.

The bar was on a skid-row street lined with shabby migratory field workers, too early for picking season, who stared vacantly at passing cars. Moss had to shoulder his way through a crowd of them to enter. Inside, the place was dark and starkly run-down. Everything of any value had been removed. No carpet, no ash trays, no lamps. All the bottles, lights, and mirrors were gathered behind the bar. Even the jukebox was down at one end. O'Malley sat at the other.

"By Jesus, there he is!" It was as if Moss, and not O'Malley, had been found.

"What are you drinkin', boy?"

"Gimme a beer." Moss sat on a padded stool next to O'Malley. The builder's breath was warm and heavy with odor like the exhaust of a rocket or a racing car. His lapels were flecked with vomit. His face was mottled, and his eyes looked like melting wax. It was as if he'd choked or been strangled and had barely survived.

"Well, I don't need to tell ya, I been on a toot. Started the night after you left. I had the good fortune to fall in with bad company. I remember drinkin' with a one-eyed man and gettin' in a fight. It's been a helluva time."

The barkeep handed Moss a dripping schooner of draft beer.

"You've really quit?"

"Yes, lad, I've had it. Sick and tired of handing out bullshit. It was getting more and more bullshit every day. Remember how we sat around and talked at first? It wasn't like work at all. But then we went and got ambitious—both of us. And now we're selling houses, and life's ninety per cent bullshit. We're up to our necks in it, and they're throwing it at us by the bucketful, and the only choice a man is left with is: Do I duck? Well, I've ducked all the way out of the whole pile."

"Have you got another job?"

"Oh, I'll catch on somewhere. There's always an opening for a fella who can sell things. This isn't the first job I've quit, you know. Or the last. When you do what I do for a living, you've *got* to quit every once in a while, just to live with yourself."

O'Malley looked into the mirror behind the bar and saw Moss staring as if he were watching his own funeral.

I am going to be left with nothing.

"Don't look like that, Ray. I'd have quit long ago, but I had to get ahead of the game first. It wouldn't have mattered to that shyster before. But now he's losing something. He's hurting. And we can sit around and talk again."

Moss smiled but slipped quickly back into his distracted stare.

"Lou," O'Malley called to the bartender, "I'll pay up now. It's time to go."

They drove back, the car steaming in the afternoon heat. Moss continued to sulk. O'Malley, seeking relief behind a pair of gas-station sunglasses, belched and sweltered and gave off all the odors of an Asian market place.

To get his mind off his own feelings, he worried about Moss's.

"Tell you what let's do, Ray. You've made out all right for the summer. Why don't you quit, yourself, and we'll head down to Vegas. Or Mexico maybe. I have a buddy who rents fishing boats in Mazatlán."

"I'd like to, but I can't."

"Well, I don't blame you, I suppose. Make it while you can. But look out for that damn Pasquinelli. He's a bad man."

O'Malley felt himself begin to doze. He slid down and lolled his head back against the seat, preparing to greet sleep.

"Would it matter to you," said Moss, looking ahead at the traffic, "if I took over your job?"

O'Malley peeked out from behind his shades. "Now, what would you want to do that for?"

"I want to get into the building business."

A speeding semi-trailer bulged out over the white line and almost sideswiped them. O'Malley sat up so quickly it made his stomach turn over. He swore at the truck driver as he passed and muttered afterwards. Moss waited.

"You're not going back to school?"

"No. It won't get me what I want."

The builder slumped down in his seat again. "And what might that be?"

Moss had thought it over so many times he spoke as though he'd rehearsed it. "To live where I want and work at what I choose."

"That's a tall order, lad." O'Malley stopped, thinking and breathing hard. He started to say something, thought better of it, then simply added, "A mighty tall order."

"Would it matter?" Moss repeated.

"What?" Now it was O'Malley who looked faraway and distracted. "No." He thought again and winced. "It'll be just what that shitty shyster lawyer wants."

O'Malley made a grinding noise with his teeth. Words and thoughts, unspoken, passed between them.

Soon they pulled even with a girl driving a motor-cycle with a black-bearded man clinging to her back. It made them both laugh.

"What the hell," said O'Malley, "maybe I can put in a bad word for you."

The car began to overheat, and Moss took a freeway turnoff that led to a service station. Rusty water boiled over the radiator when he removed the cap. The engine cooled, and Moss sipped a Pepsi; O'Malley took a long time in the rest room.

"Must be a little rusty inside, meself," he called in a jaunty voice as he came out.

Silence made O'Malley uneasy. And when they got under way again, he began passing along information about his job that he thought might be useful, like a man rummaging through a suit he's about to hand down to a brother or a friend.

"Now, all that paper work on my desk. Camouflage, that's what it is. A messy desk discourages people from nosing into your affairs, and they can't tell how busy you are either. I wouldn't touch a thing, if I were you, until someone comes in and asks, 'Where's this?' Then let him cool his heels while you look for it, and he won't be back in a hurry."

O'Malley chuckled with satisfaction. Road signs and people in other cars seemed to remind him of things.

"Don't ask for more money. Demand it. Giving up your future and all that crap. You've got to have a license. Pasquinelli will arrange it, the miserable bastard."

Moss became suddenly anxious. O'Malley was packing up and pulling out before his eyes.

"Where will you be?"

"Hell, I don't know. Loose Angles, maybe—some big developments down there. You'll hear from me. Maybe we'll hook up again sometime."

"There's something else," Moss began with difficulty. "You said you got fed up with the job."

"Indeed I did, lad."

"But the worst part of it—when you talked with people to close the deals. I saw you. I heard you. The things you said. And you *enjoyed* it."

O'Malley hid his forehead behind his hand, the knuckles white and strained. "Don't you see, boy?" His voice was sad, self-loathing. "I do. That's why I've got to quit."

They rode on in silence until they came to the outskirts of the town. As they passed along the sleepy main thoroughfare, O'Malley began muttering disgustedly at the people on the streets. The muttering seemed to revive him, as though an engine inside him were turning over. As Moss's car lumbered by the courthouse, the builder shouted.

"Whoa! Right back where I started." He pointed to a bar across the street from the courthouse. "You sure you don't want to go to Mexico, lad?"

Moss shook his head sadly. O'Malley untied the door

on his side, opened it, got out, and leaned his head back inside.

"Good luck to you, Ray. I hope what you want is worth wanting."

In a slow thick-legged trot, he ran across the street. A trucker stood on his brakes to avoid hitting him, and they exchanged insults. A fat woman stopped and gawked from the sidewalk. O'Malley strolled innocently past her, goosed her, then ran inside the bar.

Part Two

I

To the people of the town, the opening of the County Airport was an urban puberty rite, a kind of collective coming-of-age. Local merchants had decorated their stores weeks in advance; the paper put out a special progress edition; and the schools declared a holiday.

Pasquinelli made the dedication speech in a thin, piping voice that a public-address system bounced off the distant wall of a hangar and turned into a distorted echo. The wind spun his tie about like a pinwheel and splayed his hair wildly, and he kept confusing the flapping of the bunting around the speakers' rostrum with the badly timed applause of the crowd.

The airport occupied land that Pasquinelli had leased to the city, and it was named after his mother.

It occurred to Moss that in just three years Pasquinelli had grown old. Moss sat on the platform as a member of the school board, but most people there knew him better as Pasquinelli's trusted assistant and the town's bright young man. This big, amiable fellow had chosen to grow with them, and since there was no doubt that he had a promising future, it must mean they did, too. There was enthusiastic applause when he was introduced.

Congressman Bandettini snipped a ribbon across the main runway as four Navy jets roared over at treetop level, making the crowd gasp. There followed a race by the owners to the dozen or so private planes lined along the apron to see who would make the first take-off. Moss, Pasquinelli, Buddy, and Russ were in the last plane to leave.

Russ was at the controls, proudly displaying the new skill that almost made up for his game leg. Up here he was the equal of any man, and his Ryan Navion was the best ship in town.

Pasquinelli stared out at the familiar landmarks shrinking beneath them, beside himself with excitement and pride. Then, beyond the town, Russ banked, still climbing, and the lawyer lost track of everything.

Below them now was a large stretch of pale earth, dotted with featureless dwellings and crisscrossed by streets that met at rigid right angles. The houses had the drab order of cars in a huge parking lot that move away one by one until only an empty and lifeless surface remains.

"What's that?" said Moss, astonished at its vast ugliness.

"Rancho Estates," called Russ over the sound of the engine.

"It's us!" shouted Pasquinelli, peering out proudly.

Russ circled the plane over the development, and Moss stared down at row after row of look-alike homes. From the air he could see how people frequently got lost on their own street and occasionally entered the wrong house.

You build and sell them one at a time, and you don't realize how it all adds up.

"This is terrific!" said Pasquinelli, his eyes glittering. He punched Moss in the upper arm. "What do you say, Raymond?"

"Terrific."

"Go around again! Go around again!" He was like a

child on a merry-go-round. And Russ began another slow circle.

They stayed up for almost an hour and never got more than a few miles out of town. At Pasquinelli's insistence, they circled the tract again and again, identifying this building, then that one, swooping low, then climbing to see it all like a map. When at last they landed, Pasquinelli was limp and trembling, and he took both Russ's hands in his.

"Thank you. Thank you. This has been the most wonderful day of my life."

"Thank *you*, Mister Pasquinelli," said Russ. "I owe a lot to you; why, even this plane . . ."

Pasquinelli raised a hand to stop him. "No, no. Here's the man we should both thank." And he reached up and put his arm around Moss, who shrank from the man's touch.

"It's true, Raymond. I would have lost all I own if it hadn't been for you." He was sinking into mawkish sincerity again, the mark of a ruthless man grown old.

Moss started walking toward Pasquinelli's car. "Would you like me to drive?" he offered.

"No, no," Pasquinelli answered, tearing himself away from the others and following after Moss, "I'll drive."

He had always been a poor driver, and his slowed reflexes made him worse. He started the car, put the automatic shift in reverse, and they lurched backwards as Moss looked about nervously. Then he shifted into drive and headed out of the dirt parking area, narrowly missing other cars.

"I meant what I said, Raymond. You know what kind of shape we were in when that fellow left: a bank loan due and bills outstanding. You learned faster than I ever hoped you would, and you showed us what that project could become. One small tract was all I thought this town could support. Now we've bought and built up all our options, and there are more people living in Rancho Estates than there were in the whole town when we started; did you know that?"

"Yes, I did," said Moss.

"I never would have believed it was possible. Oh-oh, now we've caught the traffic."

The increased size of the town meant the two-lane main street was always crowded, and as Pasquinelli moved slowly ahead in awkward stops and starts, he talked about putting more pressure on the state assemblyman to get a freeway put through.

Moss knew it all without listening; he had heard it so many times before. He sat wondering if Pasquinelli really knew how close they had come to going under.

At first Moss had had a desperate confidence about the job; he would succeed because he didn't dare fail. But the move from the front of O'Malley's desk to the chair behind it had put him in a situation more subtle and bewildering than he could have imagined. He had attacked the job with all his energy, spending long hours at work, often indiscriminately, willing to burn himself up in an all-out attempt at success. It proved to be like trying to run on ice.

He spent most of those days with the telephone like an extension of his hand, warm to the touch, ringing whenever he set it down. He talked to prospects, haggled with suppliers, argued over ads, listened to endless advice from Pasquinelli. His presence was demanded in half a dozen places at once; four different people had left messages for him to call; or he had a week's worth of details to attend to in an afternoon.

Moss tried to do it all, and one morning he got out of bed in the rooming house and found his hands were shaking uncontrollably. He couldn't dress. He climbed back into bed and spent the rest of the morning staring at the water stains on the ceiling and sweating. He couldn't look at his hands. Eventually, he fell asleep; and when he woke again, the trembling had stopped. He showered and went out and had four drinks in the bar where O'Malley had vanished. And then he drove out to the project, threw his phone in a wastebasket, closed his office door, and admitted the people who had come to see him, one by one. And when the afternoon was over, he'd accomplished no less than he did in an average working day. After that he kept his door closed and hired a secretary to keep people out and take all incoming phone calls. He soon realized that he'd made an important business discovery. He discounted the urgency of every request, and those things that were important got done more carefully, while many things that were unimportant were not done at all. Part of his work became more manageable. There was no deadline so rigid that it couldn't be extended. Or no man so impatient that he coudn't wait. All people really seemed to want was a hearing. And Moss always gave them that.

Pasquinelli missed a stop sign at an intersection, and a kid in a delivery truck shouted at him, "Hey, pop, can't ya read?"

But Pasquinelli didn't seem to notice. He drove on, still complaining about traffic congestion.

"Vincent," said Moss, "let me out at the office, will you?"

"You're not going home?"

"I have some work to do."

"Today? Can't it wait?"

"No. I have to file some deposit slips."

"You work too much. You know that, don't you?"

"Maybe. But where would we both be now if I didn't?"

Pasquinelli stopped, thought, nodded. Nowadays kids had all the answers. It used to be that people came to him for advice and listened to what he had to say. Now the young ones paid him no mind, and they always seemed to get the last word.

"You're coming for dinner tonight, aren't you? With your lovely wife?" In Pasquinelli's small-town courtliness, every man's wife was lovely.

"I'm sorry, Vincent; I can't. I'll be here for hours."

They had turned into the street where the project had begun. All the houses were occupied now, a few by second or third owners. There were lawns and gardens and a few puny trees, and a gang of young children on tricycles or roller skates teased one another noisily at the middle of the block. Moss's car, sagging with age, was parked outside the office.

"I don't know why you keep that thing," said Pasquinelli as he pulled to an uncomfortably close stop behind it.

"It runs," said Moss, "and it's paid for."

"Buy a new one. You won't be out of a job tomorrow."

"You never know," said Moss. He opened the car door and started to get out.

Pasquinelli grabbed the sleeve of his coat. "Raymond, a man who worries all the time about losing everything usually does."

Moss stopped and, turning, looked surprised, then thoughtful. It pleased Pasquinelli that he had been able to make a point to a young person. When he drove away, he was humming.

For the second time that day, Moss felt a strange, dull recognition of himself, as though he had been watching the reflected image of a hand or a shoe for a while, and then it had gradually occurred to him that the hand or shoe was his own. He didn't want to see or talk to anybody.

He walked slowly up to the door of the butter-colored house that had never been anything but an office. Inside, the carpet was worn, the furniture scuffed and threadbare, the rooms crowded with filing cabinets, rolled blueprints, framed photographs, and stacks of brochures. Each year Moss had vowed to move to more businesslike quarters, and each year he had been too busy to do more than talk about it. Now he would have to do something; the place was really getting run-down.

He went to his desk, dropped into the chair, and waited for nightfall; and when dusk ended, he sat in the dark and listened to the crickets.

The day he had received his certificate from the state real-estate board, Pasquinelli had driven out to the project and taken him to town for lunch. While they ate, Pasquinelli was full of congratulations and suave good fellowship. Then, over coffee, he had turned cool and hard as metal. The sale of the houses had dwindled, and they were in trouble. Pasquinelli had signed a deed of trust; the bank owned everything. If the payments weren't made, they would foreclose. Did Moss have any idea what was the matter?

Moss explained that people still came out to see the houses, but they didn't buy.

"Because you can't close the deals." Pasquinelli had

said with a cold finality what they both knew was true.

He had told Moss that, since he was now licensed, he would be held accountable for every prospect that was lost. Unless Moss could show results, they would have to bring in someone else.

Pasquinelli's full, moist lips had drawn tight beneath his mustache. This was life, he reminded Moss, not school.

And so it became Moss's turn to sit and wait, as O'Malley had, for the people to be brought before him.

They were mostly country people at first. The men, deeply tanned to the neckline and wrist, occasionally flashing bits of leg as white as fish bellies, wearing plaid wool shirts whatever the weather, often cinched at the neck by a cord and sliding silver clip with a name like a number on a claim check. The women, unfinished, as though rushed out of a kitchen where there was never enough time; the children in jeans or cotton dresses, sitting quietly and staring.

They spoke slowly, with a lot of nodding and shrugging; and they were all either quietly polite or silently stubborn.

To each prospect Moss explained the advantages of Rancho Estates, described the prestige location, pushed the quality of the homes, and mentioned the likelihood that they would rapidly increase in value. He talked about the new schools that were planned and the shopping center and the healthful surroundings that were ideal for small children. It got him nowhere. Sales lagged. The harder he worked, the more he wanted to make a sale, the worse he seemed to do.

Often Moss could tell by a man's eyes exactly when he'd lost him. Sitting across the desk from Moss, the prospect would withdraw as if behind a glass, still looking at Moss, but watching the motions of his talk without hearing the sound. Moss could see the glass come between their eyes and his; he could feel them take leave of him. But he didn't know why they went, nor could he bring them back. At times he felt like grabbing them, those stringy country fathers, and shaking them till their teeth rattled. Or yelling at them. Or insulting their dull wives. Anything to bring them back. They were going to cost him his job. His future. His dream. The pressure boiled up inside him until it equaled that which Pasquinelli was applying from without.

They think they've got problems. What about mine?

He quit talking and listened.

In came Russ with a man, his wife, two children, and a grandmother, all in sunglasses, like a family of the blind. Grandma did the talking; that meant she was the one with the money.

"I've lived near the courthouse for thirty-two years and never saw anything like it. Garbage, broken glass, filthy words written on the fences. It's the Mexicans, you know."

They were always sure what they *didn't* want in a house. And much less certain what they did want.

"You won't have that problem here," Moss assured them. "This is a new neighborhood. Very exclusive."

"You mean no spics?" said the man, and looked considerately at his mother.

"I mean *very exclusive*," Moss repeated.

There was a sudden relieving shift, as though each person in the room had moved to a more comfortable position in his chair. Soon they were talking down payment and terms.

Buddy brought in a farm-machinery salesman with a

freckled face and retreating red hair that made him look like a victim of rust.

"Where do you live?" Moss asked him.

"I'm formerly from Washington, D.C.," he answered snobbishly. "Decided to grow up with the country. I need work space at home and quiet. I do a lot of writing. What about these homes of yours?"

"We call them junior estates," said Moss, and the man brightened with interest, "for young executives on the way up."

The redhead gave Moss an inside nod of recognition and moved closer.

A man and his wife, small and timid as two birds, stepped up and stood nervously until Moss asked them to sit down. They had a son who was being beaten up regularly at school. They wanted to transfer him, but they couldn't change schools without changing school districts.

"We're going to have our own school here at Rancho Estates soon," said Moss. "I'm on the school board myself."

The man and woman looked at each other and smiled, reassured.

Find what's bothering them. Find what's driving them out of their homes.

Moss waited. He listened, and he learned. He began fitting his tretament to the prospect, adopting a kind and confiding manner with one buyer, turning brusque and businesslike with the next. He admitted faults; he denied them. He joked and scolded. And when a man began to look out a window or stare down at the carpet, Moss knew he had him. He really put it to him then.

He began to sell houses.

A strange thing happened. The tougher a sale, the

more Moss began to enjoy it. Selling a man a house when he was uncertain about—or even opposed to—the idea left Moss exhilarated. Like a hunter, he rejoiced in his toughness, his lack of sentimentality, his skill. It was a physical more than a mental reaction. Moss sensed adrenalin racing through his blood; his palms tingled with sweat. He had won. Someone else had lost. He would get his way. He would succeed.

Oh, now and again there were people who would get sore at him and walk off, but they could never find words to express the way they felt. Those people never left Moss with any feelings he couldn't immediately dismiss. Except once.

There had been an old man, white-haired but erect, a grower of fruit and walnuts, whose children had married and whose wife had died. He had sold off most of his property and was looking for a house that would require a minimum of care. He told Moss that the project houses were poorly constructed, and Moss climbed all over him and bawled him out. What did he know about it? These houses bore seals and awards and warranties from some of the most distinguished insurance firms and appliance sales organizations and electric associations in the United States. Engineers and underwriters guaranteed them. Now, didn't experts like those know more about how a house ought to be built than he did? Well probably, the old fellow admitted. Maybe men from those organizations had come out and looked these houses over closely, as he had. And he didn't have their know-how; he admitted that. All he had was a little common sense. He had built his own home, you see, had cut and shaped the timbers, gathered rock and built the foundations, raised the beams, shingled the roof. He had drilled a well and dug a septic tank. So he knew what he wanted in a house. And Moss's houses didn't have it.

"Your homes, sir," he said to Moss in a calm and gentle voice, "are as shoddy and superficial as you are."

And with his hat in one hand and his cane in the other, he quietly left.

Not a week had passed since then that Moss hadn't thought of him.

Sales continued to pick up. On most weekends the development was doing better than in the early months. They no longer drew swarms of sight-seers; the project had ceased to be a novelty. Most of the people who came out were qualified prospects. And every day Moss grew more sure-handed at dealing with them.

New business began coming to the town, as Pasquinelli had promised. Suddenly there was an electronics plant, built, fenced off, and placed under a uniformed security guard almost overnight. More slowly, work began on a beet-sugar refinery.

With this small-sized boom came a new kind of buyer, a rooted transient who looked upon his house as temporary quarters, a comfortable place to house his family until they all moved on to something or some place better. A buyer who needed a house quickly and who had no permanent plans for the one he bought—an easy make.

Moss now decided he had some room to maneuver. And when the monthly income from homeowners' payments passed the expenditures for new construction, he asked Pasquinelli to get rid of his nephew.

During his first difficult days on the job Moss had got himself into trouble with the city building inspector, a nosy, talkative little man in a plastic rain hat and a windbreaker, who had the smug assurance of someone thoroughly informed about something trivial. He came out every day to examine the construction work, poked into everything, and asked Moss questions about insulation and utility lines that Moss couldn't begin to answer. Moss would have to call the contractor, who would drop his work and come over, hopping mad at being pulled off the job. Or Moss would dig up a blueprint and try to point out construction details to the inspector, which was even worse. How had O'Malley handled the man? Moss couldn't recall ever seeing the inspector around when O'Malley had been in charge.

One morning the inspector looked through a box of construction debris and told Moss, "You got a fire hazard there."

And Moss, in desperation, called Pasquinelli and asked him to do something.

Moss didn't see the inspector again. But he knew it had cost him. Pasquinelli sent his nephew Frank out to keep an eye on things. Frank stood around the office with his hands in his pockets, his black hairline scowling down to meet his eyebrows. He stared at pictures or looked at his feet in sullen shyness. Whenever Moss or Russ attempted to talk with him, Frank answered quickly and guardedly, without looking up. His uneasiness was contagious. Once, when Buddy started to tell him a joke, Frank chopped him short. "Don't get wise," he spat without looking. And they all walked on eggs for a while.

Moss resolved to get rid of him. And when the project began to show a profit, he went to Pasquinelli and told him he'd like to see less of his nephew. Pasquinelli put Frank in the back of his law office and kept him there. Moss knew then that Pasquinelli needed him badly and that the job was his for as long as he wanted it. Or as long as he could stand it.

Outside, another Indian-summer day was cooling, like baked goods out of an oven, aromatic and distracting. The acrid odor of fields in sunshine remained long after the sun had set and the fields lay in darkness. Moss sat alone in the dark, and a part of him began to stir with yearning.

It would be picking season now, and the orchard would be heavy with fruit and sweet with odor as it had been the first time he'd seen it. Another school year was beginning, and by his own calendar he was another year older. He couldn't afford to wait much longer.

When he left the dark office, it was nearly ten o'clock, and he hadn't begun the work he'd come to do. He climbed into his old car, as shabbily familiar as old clothes, and headed to the newest section of the tract, toward home.

She was waiting for him as she always did, sitting in the kitchen with a book, keeping an eye on his dinner to see that it kept warm without overcooking. She heard his footsteps coming up the brick walk and, walking swiftly through the house, reached the front door while he fumbled with his key.

Moss kissed her, and for a moment they just looked at one another. He had never quite got used to the glasses.

"Sorry I'm late. There was some work."

"Dinner's ready any time," she said a little too politely.

Moss mixed a drink while she dished up dinner noisily. She asked him about the airport ceremony, and he began a long account of the speeches, the crowds, the

Navy jet acrobats. He wanted to tell her about his flight over the tract and share the strange feeling he'd had when he'd seen it all from the air. But he sensed that she was edgy, and he was afraid she'd fly off the handle if he talked too much.

"Carla Pasquinelli called. She wanted to know what time we'd be over for dinner."

"I told Vincent we wouldn't be able to make it."

"I wish you'd told me. I didn't even know we were expected."

"Sorry. I just didn't think of it."

"You could have phoned."

She set a plate of chicken Kiev, whipped potatoes, and baked carrots with a marshmallow topping in front of him and sat down, with smaller portions for herself.

Moss could feel her tilting toward the dark side of her that frightened and excited him. He wasn't hungry, but he ate anyway. And about halfway through the meal, she picked up her book and resumed reading.

A dog barked, a long way off, and made their street seem hushed, like country.

Moss reached out and held the hand that held the book.

"Let's go to bed. I'll make it up to you."

"Not tonight, Ray. Please?"

She read on for another line or two. Then she got up, walked to the sink, and began rinsing the dishes.

If a woman is someone to be won, Moss had won his wife by losing.

Their courtship had begun with argumentative long-distance phone calls between Moss, alone and lonely in his office late at night, and Barbara, trying to make herself heard on a dormitory pay phone over a hallway full of distorted radio music and the complaints of angry, waiting girls. She was afraid of him and told him so. That was fine with him; it meant she was thinking of him. Moss, growing more confident daily of his ability to talk his way into or out of anything, persisted as he would with a customer until she agreed to see him.

They began weekly negotiations. She, having once given him what he wanted, was determined not to let him get it again. And Moss's self-respect demanded that he do to her sane what he'd done with her when she'd been crazy.

"You only want to use me physically. You don't respect me as a person."

"What kind of talk is that? Of course I respect you."

Each weekend they made out and fondled, begged, denied, and demanded until early morning, when Moss would start the long drive back to the valley, aching with frustration, his face like a clown's from kissing, nearly dozing at the wheel; then he would go to work feeling both worn out and guilty the following day. She wouldn't give in, and it was killing him. He'd call her long distance and apologize, and they'd start over again and end up the same way. Moss couldn't give up trying. And Barbara's principles were too shaky to let her avoid the test.

Eventually he came to feel so guilty and frustrated that he could no longer live with himself. Or without her. So he asked her to marry him, and she accepted.

They were married in a sooty, brick nondenominational church in Indianapolis, Indiana, where her father manufactured an engine-oil additive. He was a beefy, pragmatic man, accustomed to disappointment from his daughter, and he was still giving Moss the fish eye when he gave him her hand at the altar. Moss's half-brother Mac had been best man. He got falling-down drunk at the reception and vomited on Barbara's father's contour chair; but the industrialist, accepting the bad with the good, had grudgingly welcomed Moss as a son-in-law, and the families had parted friends.

Marriage, instead of liberating Barbara, imprisoned her in propriety. She was an imaginative cook and a conscientious housekeeper. She was considerate toward her husband; though she was brighter than Moss, she was kind enough not to let him know she knew it. She put up with his moods and odd habits without complaining; she cared for him.

All this, however, she seemed to do out of concern for what people thought, rather than what she herself felt. Toward the more personal side of their marriage, she adopted an attitude of primness. She wore simple, severe clothing; she avoided drink; in social gatherings, when the conversation began to veer toward an erotic subject, she would silently leave the group, and occasionally the room. And when she made love with Moss, it was always in the dark, with as many clothes on as possible, and with more compliance than lust. It was never again what it had been that first time.

Moss understood that this was the part of her that had brought them together, and that it could tear them apart. It was the side of her that had broken down. When she brooded or became irritable, it set Moss to wondering what she'd been like then. Had they strapped her into a strait jacket? Wrapped her in wet sheets? Had she hacked off her own long hair? Had she ever thought of him?

Sometimes the thought moved in on him, alluring and repelling as a musky odor, that she had never really had a breakdown at all, but knew and remembered everything.

When she finished the dishes, Barbara brought a cup of coffee into the living room for Moss, and sat down in the chair across from him.

"After the ceremony, we went up in Russ's plane—Pasquinelli and Buddy and Russ and I—and we flew over the project again and again. Pasquinelli insisted. I'd never seen it all before. I'd never realized what we were building. It looks as dead as a graveyard."

Barbara crossed her legs and pulled the hem of her dress down over her knees.

"You won't have to do it much longer," she said softly.

And soon Moss was away in his daydreams, and safe.

II

They returned each fall for a football game, riding along all neat and creased in Moss's dilapidated machine, Moss in a crisp summer suit, Barbara in a high-necked dress and a tiny hat that held her hair in place like a big button.

Each year the highway widened a little, and the country shrank back, as if in distaste. Only the single stretch of plum orchard remained facing the traffic, a lone, well-kept oldster in a brash gang of gas stations and car lots. It was the only place remaining where the season showed, and seeing the green trees and changing pattern of sunlight and shade, Moss felt an impulsive desire to get out and take a walk; but he didn't. Not because Barbara wouldn't have stood for it (she'd have waited in the car while Moss hiked his fill); but because, when they'd arrived at the stadium late for the kickoff, with Moss's clothes sweated through and smudged with dust, he'd have failed inspection as they nudged along the row to their seats. They always met another couple, friends of Barbara's, a different pair each year. She would embrace the other woman and they would giggle and gossip, schoolgirls again; while Moss labored at guarded conversation with the husband, who probably knew what Barbara had once been through, and might even have slept with her himself.

And after a noisy day in the hot autumn sun and a few postgame drinks, Moss would feel wilted and rumpled, as though he'd been out in the trees anyway. He'd grow quiet, and Barbara's friend's husband would slip away to join livelier company, while Moss stood alone in a shady corner of some campus patio. If it was very warm and still, he could catch the orchard odor rising as the sun went down.

Alone with her girl friends, Barbara relaxed. She laughed aloud and looked satisfied at facing down her past.

The whole thing was an embarrassment to Moss; an inconvenience; a pain in the ass; but all the way home, Barbara was so animated and happy that he knew it was really worth it.

For some time, Moss had carried a dog-eared notebook in his inside coat pocket, in which he wrote and drew diagrams in a small, neat hand. It was mostly real-estate terminology, rough sketches of houses, layouts of streets, and amateurish drawings of plum trees— bare, in blossom, and ripe with fruit.

The tract houses were now selling faster than they could be built, and the only limits to the final size of the project were space and cost. On two sides, the tract had reached its outer physical boundaries: the town and a river. And on the other two sides the price of the contiguous acreage had shot up so high it was prohibitive. They would soon be out of land, and that would mean the end of the building. Unless Moss was willing to become Pasquinelli's administrator, that would be the time to leave.

When it was clear that they had a seller's market, Moss decided to limit construction plans and begin consolidating what had already been built. Suddenly he found himself with free time, and he began reading again, drawn now to the writing of builders and planners who seemed to have some interest in common with his own. He read Lewis Mumford and Frank Lloyd Wright and a man named Ebenezer Howard, who planned a Garden City. He frequently read all night, then watched with weary eyes as the slanting gray morning fell across the tract houses. It was only then, at dawn, or in a red sunset, that he looked at his houses with any esthetic pleasure.

Moss bought more and larger notebooks and filled them and spent more and more of his mind's time away from his job.

He put on weight suddenly, as if all his clothes had shrunk in one big wash. So he allowed himself time to walk to his office, strolling in the morning through the flat landscape along the wide streets lined with low houses.

From the sidewalk the houses varied in design and trim; there were odd angles to some of the roofs, strips of wood paneling, suggestions of gables, shutters, and latticework. But through the alleyways or over a back fence, the rear views were identical: a flat stucco wall with a flush roof and windows. Each house looked chopped off, like a measured length from a big machine.

There were never any other strollers; few people walked beyond their cars. Just blond children, standing around waiting for the school bus.

At night when Moss walked home the houses were even more alike. In each front room, behind each picture window, a single lamp glowed, to keep people outside from seeing inside, where a television set blared its frenzied, mechanical laughter.

One evening, after a slow, thoughtful walk home, Moss composed a letter to an urban planner and social critic named Peter Outchinnitov, who lived in Los Angeles:

Dear Mr. Outchinnitov:

For the past few years I have been building a development here in the valley. There are now almost a thousand homes completed and occupied, and our work here is just about done. The development is called Rancho Estates. Perhaps you've heard of it.

During this time I have followed your articles and speeches in the trade press about planned communities. I have read with particular interest your strong statements in behalf of the use of existing physical attributes of land in urban development. I couldn't agree with you more.

I am interested in undertaking exactly this kind of planned development, and I would like your advice. The parcel of land I have in mind is a plum orchard, about 160 acres of level land in an area now mostly commercially developed. I do not know if this property is up for sale or, if it is, why it has not been developed earlier. It is certainly a valuable location, with a good deal of highway frontage.

My plan is to develop this land for single-family dwellings priced between $25,000 and $50,000 and subdivided into 1/4-acre to 1 1/4-acre lots. I want to keep as much of the orchard as possible intact and in its present state, to serve as a "greenbelt" and recreation area.

What I would like to know from you is this: What do you think of the idea? Has a development ever been planned around an orchard before? What steps are taken to prepare such a plan? How is the basic design protected once building gets under way?

I will be most grateful for any advice or suggestions.

Sincerely,

Raymond Moss
RANCHO ESTATES, INC.

To which, in less than a week, he received this reply, typed in blue on pale-gray stationery with "peterout-chinnitovandassociates" without spaces or capitals embossed in a matching blue across the bottom:

My dear Mr. Moss:

I must confess that at first your bold proposal caught me rather badly off balance. The very originality of your concept gave rise to uncertainty on my part. To my knowledge, no one has ever planned a development (I loathe that word, but it is appropriate) around an orchard. Perhaps for good reason.

But in the ensuing hours, a series of vivid images passed through my mind, each related to your letter and your plan. I saw a group of children shinnying up a tree to raid it of its fruit, stuffing their pockets and blouses with its riches. I saw a woman gathering fresh plums into her apron, then walking a few steps into her own kitchen to prepare breakfast. I saw a pair of lovers resting in the shade, a lovely girl leaning back against a sturdy tree trunk, her young man reclining, his head in her lap.

Your idea had seized my consciousness, and I began to realize that I had a deep, intuitive grasp of what you have in mind—not simply the facts and dimensions of your plan, but the way you feel and dream about it. (What are your feelings on ESP? We *must* talk about this.)

In my twenty-nine years of architectural practice and social planning, few ideas have grasped my attention as firmly as yours has. I will be most interested in helping you plan its execution. Please contact me by collect wire as soon as you have purchased the property.

Sincerely,

Peter Outchinnitov

81

Moss folded the letter, put it inside his notebook, and slipped both into his coat pocket. Then he took it out and read it again. On his way home he stopped outside a row of nearly completed houses, drab as metal boxes—unfinished stucco the color of gun barrels and shiny aluminum window frames. He leaned against the pipe scaffolding and read the letter once more.

The letter was enthusiastic; yet it closed on a guarded note. Why? Probably the famous planner was pestered by cranks and visionaries. The purchase of land would exclude them. The important thing was that his idea was considered sound. It was appreciated. To Moss it was now a valuable possession, one that could be easily stolen. He said nothing about it to the people at work. He discussed it only with his wife.

She had watched the change in him hopefully. At last the job was making fewer demands upon him, and he was spending more time at home. He had long, conspiratorial talks with her about their future, and his enthusiasm cheered and warmed their whole house, like a fire on the hearth. But she hadn't realized how serious he felt about the plan until she read the letter. Seeing it in writing seemed to make it fact; it no longer belonged just to the two of them. And she began to feel, along with a genuine happiness at the change in her husband, a slowly growing melancholy about his idea, a premonition of being uprooted, a fear of risking what they had accomplished upon what was still nothing but a scheme. It made her urge caution at times when Moss thirsted for unreserved enthusiasm, and she spent much time during the day alone with their belongings, fussing over the furniture and carpeting, cleaning and polishing, decorating and rearranging as though all they owned might imminently be lost. Her happiness was not her own, but his.

"I need to get an abstract."

"What's that?"

"It's a history of the property and descriptions from deeds. You get it from the county. I wonder if they'll send one to someone who doesn't already own the land. I could write and ask."

"Are you sure you should? I mean, wouldn't that let the owner know you want to buy?"

"You're right; I hadn't thought of that."

She could feel him wanting it anyway, over her doubts.

"They might not, though. It wouldn't be like you were making an offer."

"I could do it through a lawyer. It would be a legal transaction then, so it would all be in confidence."

"I guess you could," she said, and ran a hand over the upholstery of her chair.

Moss knew two lawyers: Pasquinelli and Pasquinelli's nephew, and for a time he considered proposing the whole idea to them as a business venture. But to reveal his plan to them would be to reveal himself. He had no way to limit their interest. So he sought out a stranger instead.

His wife had a friend who had a friend, a young attorney named Berg, in the distant county seat. He was ambitious but overworked; and after talking to him, Moss was confident that Berg was too busy to investigate the possibilities of the property for himself. He accepted the job quietly, and three months later he produced an abstract from a title insurance company and wearily collected his fee.

The property dated back to a Spanish land grant, of which it had been a small part. It had been a cattle ranch, and someone had once grown cotton there. Then a man named Amadeo Bagliassissi had bought it and planted it in plums. Mortgages had been taken on the property, and all of them had been paid. It was now owned by a Miss Sabina Bagliassissi and leased, under the terms of a will, to one Matisse Bagliassissi. The property was referred to in the abstract as: "land and improvements known as the Bagliassissi Ranch."

It felt strange to think of the squat proprietor as a rancher, like a cowboy.

To the written measurements and boundaries of the abstract, Moss applied dimensions of his own. He drew a rough map, including the trees, the shed, the house, and the strange tower in the front yard. Then he traced a clearer copy and put it in his pocket with his notebook and the letter. Once, he left for work without it, and at midmorning was seized with panic that it had been lost. A quick call to Barbara ended his alarm and increased hers.

The success of Moss's business was pushing him out of it. People came to look at his houses from other cities, even other states. There was no limit to the number of buyers, but there was a limit to the amount of land. Bold and uncertain at the same time, like a man descending a steep and slippery grade, Moss took his next step. He went back to see the lawyer.

Berg was the busiest-looking man Moss had ever seen. Piles of legal papers, letters, and memos accumulated around his desk like snow. Briefs and correspondence spilled over the "in" and "out" trays of the metal box on his desk. When he opened a drawer, it moved heavily. His face was gray and drawn, his eyes circled with black as though punched by wadded paper fists, his crew-cut hair grown out shaggy because he hadn't time to get it cut. When he didn't talk, Berg chewed a pencil, a poor excavation tool for a job that could stand a shovel.

"I don't know when I can get to it," he pleaded.

"That's okay," said Moss. "Take your time. Just find out who she is, where she is, and if she wants to sell."

Moss handed him a copy of the abstract, and the lawyer hunted around his desk for a place to put it. It was like tossing a snowball at a man caught in a blizzard.

For six weeks Moss waited, impatient but apprehensive, like a man expecting a report on his own medical condition. When at last Berg called, Moss was out, but as soon as he got the lawyer's message, he made an appointment and drove all the way to the distant county seat to get the news personally.

"It's an odd situation," Berg began. He held notes in one hand and letters in the other so they wouldn't get mixed up with the stacks of paper on his desk.

"The lessor, Miss Bagliassissi, and the lessee, Mister Bagliassissi, are brother and sister. The property was left to Miss Bagliassissi by her father, who specified in his will that she must lease it to her brother for ninety-nine years. She's been contacted by people who want to buy the property, and she wants to sell. The property tax is killing her—it's all been rezoned commercial around there, you know. But her brother won't give up his lease. The owner can't sell because the tenant won't let her."

"They could be trying to whipsaw somebody into paying more money."

"Unh-unh. Miss Bagliassissi and her brother don't speak to one another. Haven't for years. I found out what I know from *their* lawyer, who handles all dealings between them.

"Legally she *can* sell the property and the lease any time she pleases. But if her brother won't cancel the lease, nobody can get him off the land. It's a mess. She's waiting for her brother to die. And he knows it."

"Nice family."

"Aren't they? There's no blood quite so bad as your own."

"Say," said Moss, tugging at his collar, "this may seem a little . . . well . . . distasteful to you, but . . . do you know anything about the condition of the brother's health?"

"No, I don't," the attorney answered coldly.

"Just asking."

Once again Moss had come to a dead end. He could make Miss Bagliassissi an offer and join the death watch, but that might only bid up the price of the property. And what if the woman died first?

"What do you intend to do now?"

"I'll let you know."

And in his desultory fashion, Moss went back to his job.

Because he was less concerned about his work, Moss was more understanding toward the people on his staff. He pushed them a lot less.

He had turned the closing of the deals over to Russ, who was now oddly right for the job. Russ's seamed, weary face, his faded green blazer, his passive manner, and, above all, his limp suited the work well. There were more than enough interested buyers now, and to them Russ seemed to have been on that land for generations, surviving Indian wars and other depredations— a man slow to anger and not to be antagonized. When a prospect balked, Russ would simply show disinterest. The customer across from him, confronted with the scarcity of houses and the overabundance of buyers, more often than not panicked and agreed to terms.

As Russ's effectiveness increased, Buddy's lessened. He had opened an interior-decorating boutique in the tract shopping center and spent much of his time there among rolls of wallpaper and shelves of knickknacks. Moss, sympathizing with his outside interest, covered for him when necessary, reminding Pasquinelli and sometimes Russ that Buddy was an extremely capable real-estate salesman, especially with women.

Moss abided. He kept part of his life for himself. Alone at night, he prowled the strange common ground of all manner of men, from Thoreau to the greediest robber baron, who seek to stretch their own skins over a portion of a world too baffling to confront whole, wandering in the dark on an unmarked path between self-realization and selfishness.

In the desert the Jews dreamed of cool groves. And planted the Promised Land with fruit trees. They knew. To live with blossoms and fruit is to become one with the land.

One night while Moss worked at his desk so late that even the distant highway sounds had ceased, and he seemed to sit alone in a house at the rim of the world, his phone rang.

"Hello?"

"Mister Moss?" It was a strange, cackling voice like that of an old, drunk woman.

"Yes?"

"This is a friend. Your wife knows everything."

"What? Who is this?" he said in futile anger. And got only silence in reply. Whoever it was was still listening at the other end. So Moss hung up. And then he began to worry.

It was almost certainly someone who had picked his name out of the phone book. A crank. A screwy old woman. Almost certainly. There were people who did things like that. Solitary drinkers, aimlessly mean. They pick a man out of the book and assume he's been messing around in something. The cowardice of it was disgusting.

That's what it was, almost certainly.

But what if it was about Barbara instead of about him? What if it was some old crone who knew her in some stark mental home, who knew what she was like then and what had happened to her? Who knew that Barbara knew?

Hating himself, Moss lifted the receiver. Silence. Whoever it was, she was still there, listening.

"All right, who is this?" Moss tried to sound tough, but the words came out shaky.

And then there was a burst of ribald, masculine laughter.

"Chrissake, I thought you'd never pick up the phone!"

"What do you want?"

"What have you got? Say, you still don't know who this is, do ya?"

"Should I?"

"Listen to him. Doesn't even recognize his old buddy. Say, are you still shilling for that lousy shyster lawyer?"

Like struck fetters, his fear came off, leaving an aching relief. "O'Malley?"

"None other."

"What are you doing calling this time of night?"

"What are you doing up?"

"Just wait till I tell you."

III

"How did you know I was married?" said Moss, trying to get comfortable in a squeaky, plastic-covered motel armchair.

"Oh, I knew. I could see it back of your eyes the day you refused to go to Mexico. You were as good as married then, boy."

O'Malley lay on an unmade bed in a bathrobe as garish as whorehouse curtains. New colors—blues and purples—had appeared in his red, raw face, like bruises showing through from inside, but his eyes still moved quickly, avid with interest. And his laugh was as loud and true as the crash of a wave.

"Any little ones?"

"Not yet."

"Good. Don't be in any hurry. They're no fun at first. All they do is squawk and shit, like little wingless sea gulls."

The room was thick and airless from sliding doors and windows that fit too tight. Periodically an air conditioner whirred some wind around inside, as though on a whim of its own.

"You've done all right for yourself, I see. I passed Pasquinelli's Paradise on the way into town. You've moved a lot of homes."

"Some new business came in. That helped a lot."

"Don't sell yourself short now. The shyster will do

enough of that for ya. By the way, what's become of the motherless bastard?"

"Pasquinelli? He's changed. He's old now and harmless."

"Don't believe it. He's fakin'. Oooh, the treacherous guinea!" He pounded his fist on the glass-topped night table.

"He's rich, isn't he?" said O'Malley.

"Oh, yeah."

"And all his relatives with him, too. You can't push popsicles in this town without those lowlifes getting a cut of every sale. I don't know how you put up with them all this time, lad. I know I couldn't. Don't really know why I put up with them as long as I did. All it did was cost me money. I've made me pile now, you know."

"You have? How?"

"Dirt. Unimproved land. Sell it and let 'em do whatever they want with it. They'll buy anything within a hundred miles of L.A.—mountains, desert, anything. Huge parcels. Thousands of acres. A few sales and you've made it. I've got all I need now, so I'm coasting. Traveling around to see all my friends. O'Malley's farewell tour, like Sarah Bernhardt."

"Well, that's great. I'm really happy for you."

O'Malley smiled shyly, a little uneasy at his own success. For a minute there was silence, as the size of their unshared experience bulked between them.

"I'm leaving Pasquinelli myself," said Moss, stepping back on common ground. "I've got a project of my own."

"Good for you," O'Malley said disinterestedly. He reached for a glass of water, then used it to wash down a pill.

"I'd like to talk to you about it. You might be interested."

"I doubt it. I've had enough of house peddlin'. All you end up with is headaches and a guilty conscience."

"This is different," Moss began.

O'Malley cut him short. "We'll talk about it."

"Can you come for dinner?"

"I was prepared to insult you if you didn't ask."

While Moss leafed through a hand-me-down magazine, O'Malley dressed in a greenish suit that stretched tight over his swollen body like a canvas top on a military vehicle.

"Is there a flower shop in this burg yet?" he asked, shining his shoes with a bath towel.

"Yes. In the shopping center."

"Good. Like to pick out a little something for your missus."

Barbara had used the whole day to get ready for company, and the house had the unwrinkled perfection of a furniture show window. A turkey roasted in the oven; a portable hair drier hummed on her head. When the doorbell rang, she ran to answer it, and the drier cord, pulled out of the socket, trailed behind her.

"Don't look!" she cried, and ran back into the kitchen.

O'Malley craned his neck out from behind the door until he saw she was clothed. Then he followed Moss inside, carrying a bunch of chrysanthemums.

"Is she a robot of some kind, Ray? I thought I saw a plug."

"Make yourself at home," said Moss. "I'll get us a drink." And he walked into the kitchen, where Barbara ran back and forth from the range to the sink.

"His voice is so *loud*," she whispered. "Has he been drinking?"

"Not a drop."

"I'll just be a minute," she said, and ran back toward the bathroom.

O'Malley was pacing the living room like a suitor with a handful of flowers as Moss brought in the drinks. He stuffed the flowers into the mouth of a brass Chinese dog on the hearth and sat heavily on the sofa with his glass.

"Ahhhrrr. First one today, and god knows I need it."

"Would you like me to show you around?"

"No thanks. I know someone who got sold a house that way. Bless this house and all in it." And he took a big gulp of his drink. "Nice place you got here."

"We bought it from Pasquinelli."

"That miserable creep . . . Oh, will you look at this!"

Barbara came in from the hallway, tall, slow, poised. She wore a black dress and small earrings that made her glasses seem appropriate, like jewelry. Her hair had the fixed softness of feathers on a bird, and she smelled of soap and perfume.

"Oh, by Jesus," O'Malley growled with enthusiasm. Both men stood.

"Is anything wrong?" Barbara asked.

"You've moved in with the wrong man, my dear," said O'Malley, taking her hand. "You should have waited for meself."

Barbara blushed and lowered her eyes.

"Gerry, this is my wife, Barbara. Barbara, Gerry O'Malley."

O'Malley snatched the flowers out of the Chinese dog's mouth and handed them to her. "I'd never have brought them if I'd known how you'd put them to shame."

She blushed again, and was angry at herself for doing it.

"By Jesus, I think I could put up with Pasquinelli myself with the likes of you at home. Are you ever attracted to more mature men, my dear?"

Barbara stammered. "Well . . . I like my father."

"The law's got you there, I'm afraid." O'Malley drained his glass. "You're a fine woman, though your taste in husbands is questionable."

Her cheeks blazing, Barbara took the flowers, turned quickly, and practically ran into the kitchen. Moss followed, to refill the glasses. And O'Malley followed Moss. While she tried to get dinner ready, they stood around the oven in their shirt sleeves, laughing and talking. She was afraid to say a word; O'Malley could twist anything into a *double-entendre*. And it didn't seem to faze Ray in the least.

It was nearly nine o'clock before they sat down to eat, and the heat and color had risen in the men's faces like liquid in a thermometer. Barbara's appetite was gone. She watched with amazement as O'Malley emptied a bottle of wine and half another, while he talked on and on. When he laughed, the whole table shook. He stamped his foot and she could feel the force of it come up through the floor. He pounded the table with his fist; he pointed, shouted, reached for things, made faces, imitated people. He was the ugliest, grossest man she had ever met.

After dessert, O'Malley loosened his tie and patted his distended stomach.

"Oh, it's good to have money! As a little fella I was poor, you know." And he glanced down with pity at an unseen youth, a younger version of himself.

"Christ, we were poor. We were so poor my mother

had to cut the bottoms out of our pockets, so we'd have something to play with."

Moss glanced uncomfortably at his wife. Barbara looked and felt faint. O'Malley guffawed.

On a full stomach, he became drowsy and reflective.

"I must have sold damn near everything that's legal in this country—door-to-door kitchenware, magazines, cars, insurance, houses, land. And kept precious little for meself. The car outside is the first I ever owned. Money just slipped through me fingers till it came in a chunk so big even I couldn't lose it. Now I've got enough, and as near as I can figure, the reason is just dumb luck."

O'Malley reached out for his water glass and knocked the rest of his wine into his lap. He stood clumsily, blotting himself with a napkin, and then weaved away toward the bathroom. With an angry, lingering glance at Moss, Barbara went into the kitchen to make coffee; it was as if the end of dinner had been announced.

When O'Malley returned, Moss had spread maps and diagrams out on the living-room floor.

"This is the project I was telling you about," said Moss, guiding O'Malley away from the table. "It's a plum orchard that I want to subdivide into lots, planned around the trees." O'Malley sighed compliantly and got down on his hands and knees among the papers.

"The place would still be an orchard," said Moss, "but a housing development, too. There'd be a minimum of cutting and filling, and we'd keep as many of the trees as possible. All the utilities would be underground. We'd have minimum setback lines for the houses, and an architectural control committee would approve the design and materials for each house."

O'Malley moved from one document to the next, pudgy and crawling like an oversized infant.

"We'd have a minumum cost of, say, twenty thousand dollars for each dwelling. And no tree could be removed or mutilated without the committee's okay. There'd be no fences between the homes, just stretches of orchard for a permanent green belt."

With a sigh O'Malley raised himself up on his knees.

"What do you think?" Moss asked him eagerly.

O'Malley hesitated. "It sounds interesting."

"Do you think it's practical?"

"Well, that depends on a lot of things, like how much the land is worth."

Moss was pressing him, wanting his approval.

O'Malley got up with great effort and sat heavily on the sofa. "I had a job once, working for a Swede who was going to build a whole city down near Riverside. He wanted to make it all like Holland, with canals and windmills and crooked little streets. Well, he started off by drilling for water and struck oil. He gave up the idea of building anything and got rich. And I was out of a job. Now, that was a plan something like this, and I couldn't say if it was practical or not. It didn't do a damn thing for me. But if he'd just put up an ordinary tract on that ground without doing any drilling, he probably would have covered all that oil over without ever finding it. He got rich, but I don't know if that was what he really wanted. He just got himself deeper into things than he'd intended."

"He had a plan and he tried it. It just turned out differently."

"It was more than that. He was a do-gooder, and I don't trust do-gooders. They set out to remake the world and leave it worse off than before. Just look at your history. It's harder to let things be. When I'm planted, I hope somebody will put on me stone: 'Here lies Gerald James O'Malley. He left things as he found them.' "

"But that's exactly what this is all about. The orchard is there now, but it'll be gone soon, one way or another. I'm just trying to leave as much as possible intact."

"But you're doing it backwards, lad. You put a tree near a house, not a house near a tree."

"And look what you get," said Moss, pointing out the front window into the darkened tract. "We destroy by building. Now if that isn't backwards, I don't know what is."

O'Malley took a deep, exasperated breath and looked around the room, pointing his short Irish nose and long Irish chin like a fireman checking exits.

Moss leaned forward in his chair and rested his elbows on his legs.

"I've wanted this since before I ever went to work for Pasquinelli. It's why I came here in the first place. It's why I quit law school to get into the building business. You wonder how I put up with Pasquinelli. If that was all! It got worse after you left; did you know that? We did so lousy the bank threatened to foreclose. Pasquinelli threatened to can me; he told me so. Then I started closing deals, the same way, I think, that you did. I looked at the people, and I was scared, and I could feel they were scared, too. I could understand that part of them. And so I said to myself: 'It's them or me. Fuck them.' And I did. And I'm still doing it now, and I'll go to work tomorrow and do it again. And the reason I can do it without quitting is because I don't care. I've got this. It's all I want. And everything." Moss didn't realize how loudly he had been talking until he stopped.

Barbara stepped into the sudden quiet, bringing a coffeepot and cups.

O'Malley watched her closely as she poured. "What do you make of all this?"

She glared at him, openly antagonistic. "I want what Ray wants." Then she turned away and walked back into the kitchen.

"You know what owning land means, Ray?" O'Malley said with his muzzle down into his cup. "Lawyers, surveyors, taxes, insurance, permits . . . When you own land, it owns you. And all it is is dirt."

"To you maybe, not to me."

O'Malley looked around again for an exit and found none.

"All right, so you're going to change the world."

"Not all of it. Just part."

"Even just part is too much. But you've made up your mind. Have you bought the land yet?"

"No."

"Have an option on it?"

"Not even that. That's the problem. The owner wants to sell the lease. Several people want to buy, and they're waiting for the tenant to die. Now, I could move in and buy the land and the lease, I'm sure; but then *I'd* be stuck with the tenant. I'd need bank money, and if I couldn't subdivide, they'd foreclose. So now I'm waiting like the others, with probably a poorer chance than they have. And I wonder if there's any way around them."

O'Malley set the papers and his coffee aside. He shook his head and pinched his nose to drive away the fuzziness. He stretched and let out a long, slow yawn. And then he sat up straight with the forced alertness of an old fighter who's heard the warning buzzer.

"Why won't the tenant move?"

"The owner and the tenant are brother and sister, and, as near as I can understand, he was left out of a will. He's refusing to budge—out of spite, I suppose. They haven't even spoken to each other in years."

"How do you know he won't quit his claim?"

"He said so. That is, his lawyer told my lawyer."

"Ahhhhhhh," said O'Malley, his face lighting up, "his lawyer."

"The lawyer is the go-between for the brother and sister. And he says the only way she could sell now is with the lease *and* the brother."

"The lawyer said that," O'Malley interrupted, "but not the brother himself."

"What do you mean?"

"Well, the lawyer may *speak* for the brother, but he *isn't* the brother. It seems to me the smart thing to do would be to go see the tenant yourself and find out what he'll take to sign a quitclaim deed and get off the property."

Moss had begun to fidget with impatience while O'Malley spoke. "What he'll take? I don't think you understand. This is a matter of principle with him."

O'Malley shifted around on the couch. He wasn't sure whether it was his own bulk or that of the furniture that was making him uncomfortable, and he pounded the cushions with his hand.

"Oh Christ, lad! Everybody will take somethin'. Where's your faith in human nature?"

"You ought to see this guy. He looks all bunched up, like a fist, and I don't even know if he speaks English."

O'Malley quit shifting. It wasn't the couch; it was him. "So much the better; he'll be easier to con. I think you ought to go see him, talk to him in a nice round-about way, and find out what he'll take."

"Come with me."

O'Malley realized then that he had talked himself too far into things. The idea meant too much to Moss; to him, it was partly a matter of nerve. O'Malley knew if he agreed, he would be agreeing to much more than a visit to a surly tenant. But to turn Moss down was to reject his dream.

"All right, lad," he said resignedly. "I'll see what you've learned from the master."

Barbara had stretched the cleaning of the kitchen into as long a job as possible. She had washed and put away all the dishes, scoured the sink and the counters, and had just finished mopping the floor when Moss came in and made footprints on it.

"Where is that Irish folk-song record? Gerry's going to teach us to jig."

She closed her eyes and took a deep breath.

"You okay?"

"Just sleepy. I think I'll go to bed."

She led Moss to the record cabinet and picked out the album he wanted. Then she wished O'Malley an awkward good night and left.

From the back bedroom, she could hear them clomp-ing about the living room to the simple, appealing mu-sic, Ray and his thoroughly nasty friend, dancing out of step and singing out of tune.

For three days O'Malley visited his friends. In the mornings he drove out to Rancho Estates and chatted with Buddy or Russ or the contractor, or anyone else who happened to be standing around with nothing to do—secretaries, carpenters, salesmen, the postman. He could talk with anyone without its ever seeming like an intrusion, for even a complete stranger realized, after a few words, that O'Malley's amiability was not being used for anything; it was simply being given away. They enjoyed him for as long as he cared to stay with them.

In the afternoons he went to the bar across the street from the courthouse, where there was another set of friends and strangers who would soon be his friends. He didn't see Pasquinelli, though he made no particular effort to avoid him.

On the fourth day Moss and O'Malley went to see the man in the plum orchard.

That whole part of the country now seemed constantly in the process of construction, as though the workmen themselves, having once started to change things, could not stop. Now the highway, newly widened, was being torn up; there were heaps of earth behind yellow wooden barricades that blocked first one side of the road, then the other. With all the lane changing, traffic along the whole four-lane highway moved more slowly than it had when there had only been a narrow road.

Among the gas stations and car lots a string of dreary indoor amusements, night clubs, bowling alleys, even an outdoor archery range, announced themselves with aggressively simple-minded neon signs.

"Heavy traffic area," said O'Malley appreciatively. "Good spot for a shopping center along here."

"It's a mess," said Moss sourly, remembering the long, inviting green wall.

The last of the ground fog had just lifted when they

came upon the orchard, leaving it fresh and moist. The trees were in bloom. In the distance the blossoms hung in the air like white mist over pools of yellow wild flowers. Closer, trunks and branches appeared, connecting the colors like the weave of a fabric. When Moss and O'Malley drew so close that they could no longer see the pattern or the shape, they were in it.

"This is no place for a fancy dresser like meself," said O'Malley, as wet, long-stemmed mustard blossoms whipped about his trouser legs. "Should've borrowed a set of big-topped overalls from one of your nail pounders."

They moved through the trees toward the house, Moss a step ahead in controlled eagerness, O'Malley eying the ground carefully and trying to keep his alligator shoes clean.

Then down one long line of trees, Moss spotted the man, at the wheel of a small tractor, watching behind as the row of sharp discs he towed bit into the orchard floor and turned it from a thickly vegetated green into a rich cut brown, like pipe tobacco.

"That's him," said Moss. And the two men headed down the aisle between the trees toward the tractor. That part of the orchard that it had already tilled looked evenly brown and fertile, as if the tractor were spreading topsoil from above rather than plowing under the green weeds and flowers.

The man handled the tractor skillfully, weaving an almost complete circle around each tree while barely glancing at it. His attention was mainly on the blades, checking to see that nothing caught them and that they did not damage any trees. It seemed strange to Moss that such a thick chunk of a man could handle a machine with such precision. It did take all the man's concentration, so that he didn't notice Moss and O'Malley approaching until they were almost next to him.

"Hello!" Moss called over the sound of the engine.

The man stopped the tractor suddenly just as he was coming around a tree. The squeaking sound ceased; the thick dust in the air began to settle. The man said nothing. He sat on his machine, its engine running, staring from beneath a sweat-stained Stetson hat, his face as numbly inexpressive as a steer's.

"We'd like to talk to you about your property. Have you got a minute?"

It all seemed very awkward, because the man was clearly busy.

There was no answer, just the even sound of the idling motor and a beastlike gaze from its operator.

"Do you think he's deaf?" said O'Malley loudly.

"Might just have trouble with the language," said Moss.

Then the man on the tractor eased up on the throttle, and the engine's idle dropped to a more acceptable noise level.

"Thank you," said Moss, his face split in an exaggerated grin. The man still stared.

"We want to talk to you about your land." He stretched out his hand to indicate all the trees around.

"Do you speak English?" said O'Malley. "*Capeesh?*"

"Gnasheet," said the man on the tractor in a grunt of utter disgust. "Canna you read? Don' you see fuckina sign? No tresapass."

Moss and O'Malley looked at one another, each hoping the other would act.

"Signore," said O'Malley, reaching inside Moss's coat pocket, to Moss's surprise. "We have a paper that permits us to be here." He held up the abstract, showing its official letterhead with the state seal. "You see—'State of California.' You're Matisse Bagliassissi, aren't you? Shut off that damn machine, and come down where we can talk."

The man looked at the paper and squinted, as though he could read the small type at fifteen feet. Then he turned off the tractor engine and climbed down from the driver's seat.

"That's a good fella," said O'Malley encouragingly. But when Bagliassissi's small, heavy-shoed feet touched the ground, he stood as stolidly as he had sat before.

"What you want?" he muttered.

"Well . . ." Moss began.

O'Malley cut him off. "I think this will interest you." And he wagged the abstract at the man. "But first of all, is there a bathroom near here?"

" '*é?*"

"A bathroom. A rest room."

Bagliassissi shrugged and pointed vaguely off into the trees.

"I'm afraid that won't do," said O'Malley cheerfully.

Bagliassissi scowled, huge stone implements moving inside his head.

"Gnasheet." He picked a denim jacket out from behind the tractor seat and slipped his enormous wrestler-sized arms into it. Then he headed away through the trees. After a few steps he turned and waved irritably to Moss and O'Malley to follow him. Like obedient children, they trailed after him through his orchard to his house, arguing strategy in heavy whispers, not knowing what he could hear or understand.

When they came to the odd patchwork tower all

painted in red, white, and blue, O'Malley stopped and stared in amazement. "Well, I'll be god damned."

"'e! 'e!" called Bagliassissi, and waved after him.

O'Malley scurried along and caught up with him. "I see you are a patriotic man, sir." He spoke loud and slow.

"I like America," the man replied, mostly to himself. "Is good country."

"My country, right or wrong, but my country!" said O'Malley proudly.

"Lan uvva da brave, home uvva da free," said Bagliassissi, as though coining a phrase.

Moss and O'Malley both nodded eagerly in agreement, and suddenly the man's potato face broke into an appreciative smile, showing teeth as strong, white, and uniformly perfect as those of a carefully chosen model in a toothpaste ad.

"Wipe you feet," he said, pointing to a pair of brush mats on the porch.

And they followed him across the porch and into his house.

The inside was cool, dark, and heavy with furnishings that had been brought from another continent and another time: ornate rugs, thick drapes, furniture made from the wood of fruit trees. Every piece was in perfect condition, like an antique painstakingly restored. But these were not antiques—just ordinary household furniture so well cared for that it had not aged in fifty years. Nothing had deteriorated here; nothing had been left to waste. The oak floor glistened beyond the edge of the unworn rug; the figurines on the piano were free from dust. It was delicate work for a big man.

Bagliassissi pointed through the kitchen, and O'Malley went away in the direction of a bathroom. Then he pointed out a chair for Moss, who sat down at a kitchen table covered with spotless oilcloth. Bagliassissi picked up a broom and dustpan and retraced their path for tracked-in-dirt, while Moss sat alone and waited.

Directly across from him was a gas stove, thirty years old perhaps, with glistening black burners above a row of unchipped white handles, and next to it a noisy refrigerator with a cooling unit mounted on top. Behind him were a sink and counter of spotless tile without a dish or glass; there was only a vase set on the window sill and filled with fresh yellow flowers.

O'Malley and Bagliassissi re-entered the kitchen at the same time from opposite directions and sat at either end of the kitchen table. Bagliassissi's face became impassive again.

"We're in the real-estate business," Moss began, loud and slow, as though clear speech alone could overcome any language barrier. "And we're interested in this property. I suppose you know that this property is for sale and that someday it will be sold."

The man removed his faded hat and set it on the table. His hair was thick and black, with only traces of gray, and the brown, burned color of his face ended at a small light band just below his hairline. He nodded with a heavy reluctance.

Moss reached inside his coat pocket and took out his wallet and his notebook. He reached inside his wallet and took out a business card, which he handed to Bagliassissi. The man stared at it, reading it slowly, as though it could fully explain the two men and their purpose.

"We want to keep this land an orchard, to save it from becoming what all the other orchards around here have become. We want to know what you would take . . . (he glanced uncomfortably at O'Malley), what it would be *worth* to you to move away, to go somewhere else."

There was a brief silence as Bagliassissi waited till he was sure Moss had finished and that O'Malley did not wish to speak.

"*Io?*" he said softly. "*Niente.*"

Moss looked at O'Malley, and O'Malley looked at Moss.

"You know," Moss said, "that everything around here is changing and that this, too, will change. All your trees and all your work will be uprooted. Wasted. Unless the property is sold to someone who cares about it."

The man looked up and shrugged, an eloquent Italian shrug.

"And there will probably be nothing left here of all you have done."

The man simply stared evenly. All this was beyond his caring, or was something he had ceased to care about.

O'Malley cleared his throat.

"You work this place by yourself?" he asked. "The house, the fruit trees, everything?"

Bagliassissi answered with a series of heavy nods.

"Is it what you'd really like to do?"

The man thought a long time, then shrugged again.

"Is there something . . . anything," O'Malley continued, "that you've wanted to do but that you've never really had a chance to do? Visit the old country? Would you like to do that?"

Bagliassissi shook his head.

"Is there a place you'd rather live?"

Once again he shook his head.

"Would you like to retire? Hunt or fish?"

No.

"Play bocce?" Moss asked hopefully.

Again he shook his head.

"We want to help you," Moss explained slowly. "We want you to be able to do what you want most. We know that you don't own this land. Probably you won't get any of the money that it will bring when it's sold. Unless you let us help you. We want to give you . . . to help you arrange things the way you want."

The man stared and began to finger his hat, eager to get back to work, where it was less confusing.

"Is there a job," said O'Malley, leaning back in his chair and peering out of the corners of his eyes, "is there a kind of work you'd like to do?"

Bagliassissi brought a thick, leathery hand like the padded sole of an animal's paw up to his mouth and thought for a long time.

"*Si*," he said finally. "I would like to be a sca-venge."

"What? What did he say?" said Moss quickly.

"I don't know," said O'Malley. "I didn't catch it."

They talked across the table as though the man wasn't there.

"What was that?" said Moss. "What was it you'd like to be?"

"Sca-venge," the man repeated. "Sca-venge."

Moss looked at O'Malley, who shook his head in bewilderment.

"Sca-*venge*," the man said slowly to Moss, exactly the way Moss had talked to him.

"Sca-*venge*, sca-*venge*," he said with growing impatience.

Moss looked pleadingly at O'Malley, hoping somehow he would understand what Moss could not.

"Gnasheet!" said Bagliassissi and got up and walked out as though in a rage.

Moss and O'Malley sat without speaking, feeling quiet press in upon them. In whispers they began to argue.

"Why didn't you leave the talking to me?" said Moss.

"You were making a mess of it," said O'Malley.

"Like hell I was. I was reaching him."

"Bullshit," said O'Malley.

Bagliassissi returned carrying a gunny sack with a suspicious fragrance. His face turned away in distaste, he swung the sack up on the kitchen table, and its contents began to roll out the open end: fruit rinds, eggshells, coffee grounds.

"Garbage!" said Moss in astonishment.

"*Si, si,*" said Bagliassissi animatedly, "scavenge."

"Sca-venge," said Moss with a glow of recognition, "scavenger . . . He wants to be a garbage man!"

"Well, I'll be god damned," said O'Malley as a lemon rind rolled into his lap.

A lifetime on the land had been one filled with uncertainties: drought, storms, lean years of hard work, rich years of low prices. The best business, to Bagliassissi, was the most consistent one. And there was nothing more certain than garbage.

"You want a job as a garbage man?" said Moss eagerly. "We'll get you one."

Bagliassissi raised his thick-skinned palm. "No, no. Scavenge is association. You have to buy."

"You have to pay to be a garbage man?" O'Malley said incredulously.

"We'll pay," said Moss firmly. "How much?"

"You buy?" And the stolid face bloomed in a surprised smile. "*Grazie.*"

"How much?" said Moss impatiently.

"*Momento.*" Bagliassissi got up and plodded out into

the hallway. As Moss and O'Malley stared at each other, they heard the man dialing a telephone. He had a short, rapid Italian conversation with someone on the other end of the line. Then he hung up and returned.

"My friend," he said, returning to difficult English and pointing a thumb over his shoulder as though someone waited in the hallway, "he's a scavenge. He come."

Then he opened a cupboard and brought out a dark, unlabeled wine bottle. "Marsala?" he smiled.

O'Malley nodded, and Bagliassissi set up three glasses.

Half an hour later, a black Cadillac pulled up outside the house, and a small, lively old man in an overcoat and a flat little hat with the brim turned up all the way around leaped out and bounded up onto the porch. He and Bagliassissi embraced, and Bagliassissi introduced him simply as Domingo. He had quick, tiny eyes that glittered against skin the even copper color of Lincoln's on a penny, and a mustache as thick and white as a tuft of cotton. His voice was high-pitched and raspy, as though he had spent a lifetime trying to make himself heard above crowds.

The four of them stood in the kitchen while Bagliassissi explained the offer in Italian and Domingo nodded attentively. Moss and O'Malley watched uncomprehendingly and with a growing defensiveness.

When Bagliassissi finished, the small man smiled, shook Moss's hand and then O'Malley's and sat down at the table behind a glass of wine. He took a sip, sloshed it about inside his mouth, swallowed, and cleared his throat.

"You wanta to buy shares?" he said. His voice sounded an octave too high, as though the attempt to clear it had failed.

"We want to buy him a job as a garbage man," said Moss. "How much?"

"Elevena thousand," said Domingo.

"What!" shouted O'Malley.

"Cash," he added with another smile.

"Eleven thousand *dollars?*" said Moss, disbelieving his ears.

"*Si,*" said the little man, still smiling. "Eesa corporation. Lika General Motors. You buya shares."

"Shares! Of garbage?" said O'Malley.

The smile vanished. "Eesa good investment. Always a profit."

Bagliassissi smiled proudly, as though already a stockholder.

"Eleven thousand dollars—cash," Moss said to O'Malley, who whistled silently and rolled his eyes.

"I don't have that much," said Moss.

Domingo and Bagliassissi frowned identically in skepticism.

"With me," Moss added quickly. He could feel himself beginning to perspire as O'Malley watched in astonisment. "But I can get it. Is tomorrow soon enough?"

The farmer and the garbage man grinned with relief. Domingo shook Moss's hand and O'Malley's, and Bagliassissi refilled the glasses with sweet wine.

"Are you off your ass, lad?" said O'Malley as the two men walked quickly through the trees. "Why tomorrow? He'll keep."

"I don't want him to see his lawyer," Moss said under his breath, though the house was already a good distance behind them. "If the sister finds out he's moving, she'll up the price. If he sees all that cash and feels it and counts it, he'll deed over his lease on the spot."

"You hang tough, lad," O'Malley said with admiration. "You've got balls on ya, no doubt about that."

"There's a problem," said Moss after he'd moved the slow, heavy car into the highway traffic. "I don't have the money. I've got maybe nine thousand in my account. The rest is invested, and I can't sell it by tomorrow."

O'Malley sat silently, reckoning. He should have guessed. "How much do ya need?" he said flatly.

"Look, I hate to ask. But I'll pay you back as soon as I can cash some securities."

"How much?"

"Well, I'd rather not clean out the account completely. . . ."

"How much?"

"Three thousand?"

O'Malley drew a long, contemplative breath. "Awright. I own a piece of a garbage man."

The document was printed on parchment, the text bordered in imitation gold leaf, headed by a thick Tudor-black title: SCAVENGERS' BENEVOLENT ASSOCIATION, and closed by a shiny gold seal. Moss read it through, noting the creed and bylaws, then signed it as a character reference. He handed the paper across the kitchen table to Bagliassissi, who balanced it on his fingertips to avoid prints, while Moss handed the cash over to Domingo.

He was $414.71 short. "Tax" was the only explanation Domingo would offer, but Moss figured it was the wily little man's commission on the deal.

Domingo accepted a check with reluctance while Bagliassissi wrote his name laboriously on a quitclaim deed, and the three men shook hands.

"I have a favor to ask," said Moss. "I would like you

to keep living here for a while, just a few weeks. And I don't want you to tell anybody that you're moving."

The other two men looked at each other suspiciously and spoke quickly in Italian.

"I don't want your sister to know," said Moss over their chatter.

And Bagliassissi smiled his big, toothy grin and winked in appreciation.

"I gotta requesta, too," he said, turning serious. "Outside my wife, sheesa grave . . . how you say?"

"Buried," said Domingo.

"Ah, *si*. My wife, sheesa bury there. You leave?"

"Of course," said Moss.

"Every day," said Bagliassissi, knotting his thick fingers and staring down at them, "I put flower there. You put flower there sometime?"

"Sure, I'll see to it."

"*Grazie. Grazie.*"

They were silent for a moment, each side waiting to see if the other had anything to add, any last request to make.

"Is good country," Bagliassissi said finally. "Where a orchard grow, doctors go broke."

IV

To Moss's surprise, the bank loan was an easy matter.

He had entered the cool, quiet bank chamber defensively, silently reciting answers to unasked questions as he took a seat beside a marble pillar and waited for the loan officer to see him. Even this small-town branch had the big bank's air of great and remote power very seriously administered. But when the bank guard swung open the low gate in the counter and beckoned to Moss to enter, and Moss felt the marble floor turn to carpet, his desperate confidence returned. They were in business, as was he. He had a deal; they would be interested.

The loan officer was a frail, balding man with thin, widely spaced hair that appeared to have been raked into place with a garden tool. He listened closely, with his hand held up to his mouth as though withholding comment, while Moss presented his documents and outlined his proposal. After glancing at the abstract and the quitclaim deed, a metes and bounds description, and the letter from Peter Outchinnitov, the banker seemed to lose interest in the details of the proposal and grow anxious for Moss to get to the point. And when at last Moss mentioned the figure, two hundred thousand dollars for one hundred and sixty acres of land, the man accepted it without any noticeable reaction at all. He simply removed his hand from the front of his mouth and said quietly, "I think we'll be able to work something out."

It was decided as simply as that, subject to the approval of the bank's executive officers. The banker suggested four successive loans of fifty thousand dollars, each fully amortized within six months. In accordance with state law, Moss would have to sign a deed of trust; the property would belong to the bank until it was fully paid for, and the bank could foreclose if any of the payments were not met. When did Moss expect to conclude the sale?

"Within a week or two," Moss said.

"I see no reason why you shouldn't proceed with negotiations," the banker said casually. Then, noticing that Moss did not appreciate the finality of the statement, he added, "I see no reason why the loan shouldn't be approved."

"Is that all?" said Moss, candid in relief.

"Yes. You'll hear from us." And the man's hand returned to his mouth, cutting off his own words.

Moss waited, wanting more. A wish of good luck, perhaps, or an expression of enthusiasm for the project.

Nothing. The banker put Moss's papers in a fresh Manila folder, and Moss clasped shut his attaché case and left.

Once outside in the spring warmth, he felt limp with relief. It was so easy. The orchard would be his. Along with this physical relaxation, he felt a soaring sense of his own possibilities, like a student swept up in graduation-ceremony oratory.

I'm my own man. I don't work for anybody.

By that simple piece of strategy, dealing directly with Bagliassissi, he had outwitted the others. It was as though he had won the orchard as a prize.

The preliminary negotiations with Miss Bagliassissi's lawyer had been carried out in complete secrecy. In fact, Moss hadn't even told Berg that he'd acquired the lease to the property, and the young lawyer had argued eloquently in his client's behalf before agreeing to a figure that was exorbitantly high for a plum ranch but an out-and-out steal for a real-estate development.

Miss Bagliassissi, it was said, accepted the deal with great pleasure, delighted to be free of her last legal tie to her brother.

And someone (it must have been O'Malley) left a spade, a hoe, and a box of mole poison on Moss's doorstep.

Pasquinelli would know now, Moss thought as he walked to his car. He must have relatives in the bank, as he did everywhere else. It would be a bad way to get such news, and Moss wondered how the old man would take it. He wondered for a minute or two.

When he told Barbara, she said simply, "Oh. That's wonderful," and busied herself in the kitchen repainting an enamel baseboard. But Moss was eager to talk, and he interrupted her while she was still mixing the paint.

"Do you realize what this means? I can be myself more than two days a week. I'm my own boss now. We'll have everything we want."

"Yes, it's wonderful." She was wearing one of his old shirts and a pair of Capri pants. The ordinariness of such things on this special day annoyed him.

"Is that all you can say? Can't this wait?"

"If we're going to sell the house, it'll have to look nice."

"The hell with the house! We'll take a loss. Let's go have dinner out."

"All right," she said without looking at him, and resumed mixing paint.

Moss walked into the living room and started drinking by himself. By the time they were both ready to go out, he was slightly drunk and very disagreeable.

Over an expensive, unappreciated restaurant meal, he tried to interest Barbara in his plans. He spoke glowingly of Bagliassissi's house; she worried about selling theirs. She wanted to know how he intended to break the news to Pasquinelli. And yet these things weren't really what was bothering her at all.

"Why don't you like Gerry?" Moss asked her bluntly.

"He's so . . . preoccupied with sex."

"Yes, he is," Moss agreed. Facetiously, he added, "Not at all like yourself."

Barbara stared at her plate for a moment; then she rose with abrupt haughtiness and left. Moss, assuming she'd gone to the rest room, waited a full half hour before finishing his meal alone.

Sheepishly, he paid for her untouched food, went out to the parking lot, and found her sitting in their car, apparently absorbed in the text accompanying a road map. For the rest of the evening she wouldn't say anything to him beyond a simple yes or no.

She was still not speaking to him in the morning. But Moss did plenty of talking. He called Berg and told him to make final arrangements for the purchase. And he had a long, loud, laughing conversation with O'Malley.

Barbara avoided him and spent nearly three hours operating the vacuum cleaner.

Moss fled the house at noon and drove to his office,

but there was little for him to do. Russ and a couple of the salesmen seemed surprised to see him, and Moss's presence made them shift about, uncertain whether they should shoot the breeze with the boss or look busy. Moss settled it for them by going into his office and shutting the door.

He opened a stack of letters, all circulars, inviting him to take out a credit card, be listed in a real-estate Who's Who, join a lodge, subscribe to a newsletter, attend a conference on subdivision marketing, and buy land in Oregon. How did he get on these mailing lists?

Bored and restless, he stared out his dirty window into the laundry room of the house in back. A haggard-looking young woman was loading piles of wet wash into a clothes drier, feeding the machine as though she were a machine herself.

Moss turned away, and walked out of the office and through the house. He had just opened the front door when Pasquinelli's car slowed and stopped behind his.

The old man got out, wearing a black coat and Homburg hat despite the warmth of the day, and came up the walk slowly, his arms at his sides, fists clenched as though holding suitcases packed with grief. When he looked up and saw Moss, waiting in the doorway, he made no sign, but his upper lip and his mustache moved once, quickly, in an involuntary tic that made Moss shudder.

"Hello, Vincent."

"Raymond."

"Won't you come inside?"

"Yes. In your office."

Pasquinelli led the way slowly, entered Moss's office, walked around the desk to Moss's own chair, and sat in it. He took off his hat and placed it on the desk, as if to announce who was in charge. Moss stood across the desk from him, the room strangely reversed around him.

"What's this I hear about your leaving?" said Pasquinelli, his face set and stern. Again his lip and mustache ticked.

Moss sat on the desk, narrowly missing Pasquinelli's hat. "I'm starting a development of my own."

"And you never told me."

"It was one of those things. It had to be kept secret."

"Behind my back you arranged it, while you worked for me." Pasquinelli's voice was muffled with bitterness, and he seemed to speak almost to himself.

Moss's stomach was still queasy from the night before. His head felt as though it were inside an oven. And the sight of the old man sitting in the stuffy office in a coat made him perspire all over.

Their friendship was finished. But perhaps they could be something less than enemies if Moss avoided the wrong words.

"Yes, that's true. I did it while I worked for you, Vincent. But not until my job here was finished."

"It isn't finished."

"It *is*. I'm a builder, and this place is built."

"You have a job here with me. You have an obligation."

"I've paid you back, Vincent. No one else would have worked so hard. . . ."

"You're disloyal."

"Oh, for god's sake, Vincent. This isn't the priesthood. I want to do something else. It's as simple as that."

"No, no," the old lawyer said slowly, "it's not simple. You plotted. You didn't come to me and tell me. You didn't even come to me for money."

"I didn't come to you because I want my project to be mine, just like this one is yours. Vincent, I've had this idea for years. It's like a dream, a kind of development nobody has tried before. If it's going to work at all, it has to be done my way. I have to be boss. That's why I didn't come to you. Besides, the risks are terrible. You're better off out of it. Why don't you just relax and enjoy life?"

When Pasquinelli looked up, his face had the sagging look of someone about to cry; but his eyes held no tears.

"Raymond," he said huskily, "do you know what the matter is with you? You're shallow—deep down inside."

Moss cocked an ear toward him, not sure he'd heard correctly.

Pasquinelli continued, his speech rambling, growing incoherent, like an old man ranting at empty benches in a park. O'Malley was the cause of it, Pasquinelli knew that; he'd come back to town to talk Raymond into leaving. They'd been seen together, Raymond and O'Malley.

It was the first time Moss had heard Pasquinelli mention O'Malley's name since O'Malley had quit.

Moss had betrayed him, had joined up with his enemies. O'Malley was no good; Moss ought to realize that before entering some vicious scheme with him. A man like O'Malley never amounts to anything, and he causes nothing but trouble.

"Vincent," Moss interrupted, "it's *my* idea, *my* project—not his. And as for amounting to something, he already has. He's rich."

"Ha!" said Pasquinelli in a strange, sad-faced laugh. "Do you know how?"

"Unimproved land, near Los Angeles."

"It was unimproved, all right. It didn't even exist. It was a swindle. They sold property that wasn't even there. Robbed people of their savings—that's what kind of man he is."

"How do you know that?"

"I have friends there, like here."

"It isn't true. He'd be in jail if it was."

"Not him. He'd find a loophole. Probably didn't sign anything. Or did all his business in cash. But that doesn't mean they won't catch up with him. And how will that be for you when you're in business with him?"

"It's my business," said Moss. "Not O'Malley's. And not yours."

"I know that man, Raymond. You don't. If you knew the truth about some of the things he's done . . ."

"Vincent, is that what you'll say about me when I've gone?"

"What? What do you mean?"

"That's what really bothers you about O'Malley, isn't it? That he quit. Left you. And now it's me. So now I'm on your shit list, too. Isn't that it really? Won't someone else be sitting here where I am with you telling him about that 'Moss, who was no damn good'?"

"Raymond . . ."

"How much notice do you want?"

"Raymond, don't. Listen to me."

"Two weeks? A month?"

"I'll finish you in this town, Raymond."

"I'm moving."

"You won't ever be able to come back."

"Two weeks ought to be enough. I recommend Russ as my replacement. He's already doing my job anyway."

"You're throwing your life away." He mumbled on, threatening and resentful, until Moss made him listen.

"Vincent. Vincent! *Vincent!* Thank you for saying what you did. You've made it easier for me to leave."

Moss held out his hand, knowing Pasquinelli would not take it. And then he left the old lawyer slumped in the chair, the collar of his overcoat up around his chin, sitting behind the desk where two men had become his enemies.

They closed the sale a week later—Moss, Berg, and Miss Bagliassissi's lawyer, whom Moss treated rudely because he was old and Italian and reminded him of Vincent Pasquinelli—seated close together in Berg's cramped office.

Moss handed Miss Bagliassissi's lawyer the bank's check for fifty thousand dollars, and the lawyer handed him a land contract in return, granting Moss possession of the property and agreeing to give him the deed upon completion of the purchase payments.

Once he touched and held the contract, Moss didn't hear another word that was spoken in the meeting. His dream was fact.

Soon they were in the hallway shaking hands, and then the two lawyers dashed away in opposite directions to equally pressing appointments, leaving Moss alone with his prize.

Aware only that he was driving, Moss headed unconsciously toward the orchard, poking along slowly in the slow lane, people honking horns at him and pulling out to pass. And then he was there.

It was a sunny, cold winter day, so clear and still that there was no trace of fog or smoke, and even the normal distortions of depth and distance were gone. Every object for miles stood out with perfect shape and color, each branch on each tree in each row, and the hills and mountains beyond, with the precise unreality of stage scenery.

It was his: this orchard, this grove, this peaceful place.

Moss stood in the chill shade, savoring the feeling of time and distance thwarted. All was now as it had been in this sequestered place, remote from everything around it. The endless files of trees were perfectly aligned whatever perspective he took—a colonnade, a maze, infinity.

He ran his hand along a tree's rough gray bark. He picked a bouquet of yellow mustard flowers from a patch of orchard floor not yet tilled under. And he walked slowly through the trees, feeling the soft soil give beneath his feet in the alternating warmth and cold of winter light and shadow.

And when he reached the house where he would live, he walked slowly around it, as though taking possession from the outside, past the garden and the tool shed and the smooth, rounded mission angles and corners of the house itself.

He stopped at the gaudy, peeling monument and searched for a headstone without finding one. Then he tucked his handful of wild flowers in a red-white-and-blue abalone shell that must have been put there for the purpose.

When Moss got home, Barbara told him she was pregnant. There was nothing left, that day, to wish for.

Part Three

I

A week after they had moved into the house, it seemed as if they had always lived there. There was a place for everything, a hinged cabinet for the ironing board, a niche for the telephone. Even the inconveniences, like the furnace, which had to be adjusted from the cellar, seemed familiar. And the foundation, Moss noticed, was made of whitewashed adobe, sun-dried brick, as though the house itself had grown out of the earth that supported it.

For a time he dawdled, puttering about the tool shed and the trees, enjoying things as they were, as if he owned them. Then O'Malley warned him to snap out of it.

"Look, lad, those bankers may be nice, agreeable fellas when they grant you a short-term loan. But they freeze up when it comes due. Believe me, if you don't know what to do with this place, they will. Get busy."

He should start by getting his land surveyed, said O'Malley. And checking into the local zoning ordinances. And the water supply. And sewage-disposal arrangements. He should look into the matter of entrance streets and storm-water outfalls. And utilities.

By the time O'Malley had enumerated the things that must be done, Moss was anxious with guilt. He went directly off with O'Malley to see a surveyor and sent a wire, as requested, to Peter Outchinnitov.

Two days later, while the surveyor was peering

through his telescope at an assistant holding a graduated pole, a great noise passed over them, a whirling pop and thud, sucking up dust and casting a moving shadow on the ground. A helicopter hovered noisily above the house, then landed lightly in the front yard, just next to the monument. Two men got out: one bearded and loaded down with photographic gear; the other, silver-haired, with a mustache to match, wore a tweed jacket, an ascot, whipcord riding breeches, and boots polished to a high gloss.

"Mister Mouse?" the silver-haired man said, addressing himself to O'Malley. "I am Peter Outchinnitov."

He stood as though posing for sculpture, with one hand tucked neatly in his coat pocket, the other free to gesture. And he spoke with an indefinable accent that made him sound not just foreign but imported.

Moss stepped forward with an awkward formality. "I'm Raymond Moss."

"Ah, good," said the silver-haired man. "And this is my ay-eerial photographer, Steinbrunner."

The photographer looked up with a thin, brooding face, then peered down into a light meter.

"There is much to be done here. But first we shall have tea, no?"

"Sure. Right this way," said Moss. And he led them up onto the porch.

"I want to name the streets after the different varieties of plum," said Moss. "Santa Rosa, Mariposa, Duarte, El Dorado, Wickson, Tragedy, Becky Smith, Queen Ann, Kelsey, Laroda, Nubiana . . ."

"Good, good," said Outchinnitov after a moment's reflection.

Along with his imposing appearance, he had an unsettling way of looking at others intently until they felt obliged to speak, then seeming not quite satisfied with whatever they said. It made people want to prove themselves to him.

"This must be a whole community in an orchard, not just houses with a few trees around them," Moss added. "You prepare a plan for me, and I'll see it through. I won't knuckle under."

Then O'Malley felt obliged to speak. "Before you can start grading, you have to submit a general plan to the county planning commission. If you wanna keep the bank off your ass, you better hop to it."

Peter Outchinnitov glanced at O'Malley with cold distaste. O'Malley smiled and winked at him.

Moss started again, as though jumping between them. "Mister Outchinnitov, how do I get this place zoned the way I want?"

Outchinnitov set his cup and saucer on the low porch table, and, in doing so, turned his back on O'Malley.

"You cannot. Zoning protection is limited to police powers. Public healt', safety, and welfare." He paused a moment and looked around at the others on the porch: Moss, tight strung, with a gray cast to his skin, perched on the edge of his wicker chair; Steinbrunner, glancing nervously up from his tea at the distant hint of clouds; O'Malley, slumped inertly in a rocker with only his jaws moving, busy with a piece of gum. Outchinnitov looked at each of them, letting them know for sure who the man was with all the answers.

"Protective covenants can accomplish much more. I will draft you a set."

"Great," said Moss.

"Using the ay-eerial photographs we are taking today, we will build a complete topographic model of your property in my studio, where I and my staff shall study it. From this model we will prepare the master plan. This will be a book, handsomely produced, with actual mock photographs of the completed development. The plan will include building types, price range, typical lot size, streets, right-of-way and roadway widths, grades and gradients, easements, storm-drainage system, lot lines and numbers, minimum building setback lines, key plan, legend, notes, and site data."

"When will we have it?" Moss asked.

"In one month. You can telephone my unlisted number if you have any questions. And if you wish, I will present the master plan myself to the planning commission."

"Good. I think that will be very helpful," said Moss.

"How much?" said O'Malley. And Peter Outchinnitov's mouth and mustache curled down in displeasure.

"Fifteen thousand dollars."

O'Malley whistled. Moss swallowed hard and nodded.

"We must begin with a survey."

"I've already started. In fact, the surveyor's at work now."

"I am sorry to hear that," said Outchinnitov. "I must have my own surveyor. It's quite impossible for me to work with someone else."

"What do we do with the man we've got?" said O'Malley.

"Fire him," Outchinnitov said coldly.

They sat on the porch talking most of the afternoon. About four o'clock the pilot came up from the helicopter, where he had been sitting patiently for hours, and warned them that it was going to cloud over before long, and if they wanted to get any decent pictures, they'd better get started.

After Outchinnitov groomed himself inside the house and the photographer gathered up his gear, they took off, floating up backwards as though in a reversed film. Moss and O'Malley remained on the porch, watching them pass back and forth overhead, the photographer pointing a long, fat lens down at the property like the muzzle of a cannon.

"What do you make of him?" said O'Malley.

"Oh, I don't know," said Moss reluctantly, "a little flamboyant and opinionated maybe. But after all, that's what he's selling—his style, his way of doing things. And he's a good salesman, no doubt about that."

"It looks like some sort of art con to me," said O'Malley. "All this stuff about civic opportunity and creative instinct has a hollow sound to it, if you ask me."

"Who's asking?" said Moss.

O'Malley looked at him, then nodded slowly to himself.

"I guess I'd better go tell the surveyor that he's been fired."

At first Barbara had feared the house would be more work than she could handle. The inadequate wiring, for example, made many of their appliances useless. But washing the few dishes they used proved to be little more work than scraping them clean for a dishwasher, and the task itself took on more meaning when it was left completely up to her. And there were other compensations. Their laundry, which in the past had been spun-dried in a clothes drier, she now had to carry outside and pin on a clothesline; but when she took it down, each piece smelled of fresh air and sunshine instead of detergent, so that putting on clean clothes was like bringing the outside indoors. Each evening they had a large and fragrant fire on the rock hearth. And she felt her own strength growing with the life inside her. For the first time in a long while, her wishes seemed to be intertwined with Raymond's, and when she mended socks or sewed buttons, she sometimes found to her surprise that she was completely absorbed in these simple household tasks. She did wish that Raymond could be more concerned with the baby; but perhaps that, too, would come with time. Because she kept so busy, it was easy for her to keep her weight down, as the doctor insisted.

There was only one bad part to it all. Every time Gerry O'Malley saw Barbara, he gave her swelling figure an appreciative glance that, wherever she was and whatever she was doing, made her feel absolutely naked.

O'Malley had a crony at the county development office, an old newspaperman who now held down a post that was half real-estate promotion and half public relations. He fed O'Malley information about local land values and ordinances, and he also told him something about the official personalities who would have to give final approval to the project.

"They're mostly political appointments," O'Malley told Moss one evening as they both sat, legs outstretched toward the fire. "A couple are old-timers who got rich off their land and have plenty of time to spare, and a couple are newcomers who're getting rich now and don't have time for anything. They all seem to go along with the chairman. Man named Stragan, ex-Marine major. He's ambitious, wants to hold elective office, so he leans on the local mayors from time to time, looking for soft spots. You weren't ever in the Marines, were you?"

"No, Army."

"Too bad."

"I think we'll handle him," said Moss. "If he's ambitious, and we can explain to him what this development means in terms of the county's future, he'll probably be on our side. Do you realize that what we're doing here could be of nationwide significance?"

O'Malley looked thoughtfully into the fire.

"Have you any relatives who were Marines?"

The following day a Chinese boy who appeared to be no more than fifteen years old drove up in a dusty station wagon and unloaded an odd-looking box mounted on a tripod. The boy was abnormally thin, with a thick, weedy growth of unmanageable black hair that made him seem top-heavy. He wore a slide rule attached to his belt that was longer than the width of his waist, and he introduced himself as Peter Outchinnitov's surveyor. The land would be surveyed, he said, by radar.

That afternoon he moved about the property setting up the box at different points in the orchard and peering at it through another box set upon another tripod. Mounted on the first box, apparently some kind of transmitter, was a metal dish about the size of a salad bowl with a metal cone inside, pointing out. By moving these two pieces of equipment around the orchard, he completed his survey that afternoon; and half an hour after he announced that he was finished, he had loaded his equipment back into the station wagon and was gone.

Almost daily, memos "From the desk of Peter Outchinnitov" turned up in the project's thickening pack of mail. Each memo was merely a brief question, such as "Water?" or "Transportation?," above the simple signature "P. O." Through his friend in the county administration, O'Malley would gather all the local information on each subject requested; then he and Moss would condense it into a report and mail it to Outchinnitov by nightfall.

O'Malley's friend also briefed him on the proper procedure for submitting a subdivision plan to the county commission. A copy of the plan was to be submitted in advance to Stragan, through his secretary. At that time an appointment would be made for a hearing.

At O'Malley's suggestion Moss prepared a subdivision report showing that he had clear title to the property and submitted it to the state real-estate commission. A copy of such a report, issued by the commission, could be a big help in winning over skeptical buyers.

O'Malley also told Moss to take out an insurance policy on the development and enclose a copy with his report, which Moss did.

And when the question of a contractor popped up, O'Malley had just the man in mind—Reese, the temperamental man from Rancho Estates. The contractor was delighted to get the job. Pasquinelli, he said, had taken over management of the development, and working with him was even more maddening than working with Moss. When the contractor came to look over the new property, he and O'Malley greeted each other like old war buddies.

His continuing dependence upon O'Malley annoyed and frustrated Moss, and he felt increasingly sensitive about asking the older man for advice. O'Malley, aware of Moss's touchiness, continued to counsel him anyway, realizing that with all Moss had staked on the project, and with a baby on the way, he could not afford mistakes.

Several times Moss had offered O'Malley a salary, and each time O'Malley had refused. "Pay the bank off first," he insisted. But one night, after a long swim up a stream of steak-house Martinis, Moss prevailed upon him to accept a monthly retainer as a consultant. This accomplished two things as far as Moss was concerned: it allowed him to make some gesture of paying off his indebtedness to O'Malley, and it defined his position, so that there was no doubt as to who would make the decisions. Inadvertently, it also put their friendship on a more businesslike basis.

It was at about this time that Moss first began to receive offers for that part of his property that fronted on the highway. Apparently, word had leaked out that the orchard was going to be subdivided, and commercial developers began to write and call. Eager to locate near a new residential area, they made increasingly extravagant offers for highway-frontage lots. Moss's reluctance to discuss any such sale only served to bid the offers up even higher, and pending the completion and approval of the master plan, he could not give any commercial builder a final "no."

And when the letters and the phone calls and the waiting and planning got to be too much, there was still the orchard.

The first morning that Barbara put on a maternity dress, Moss took her for a walk among the trees. The early spring blossoms were all but gone, and bits of green leaves were just beginning to show through the bare branches, as though they'd been waiting fully formed inside all along.

Still slender, but firm-looking, in a cotton shift she'd

made herself, Barbara walked barefoot down an aisle, arm in arm with her husband. And when they came to a last, full-flowered bough, still white and fragrant, and Moss reached up to break it off, she called out to him, "Ray, don't."

"If we take it home, it'll keep for a couple of days."

"Please don't. Let it live."

With a loud snap Moss broke the branch. And Barbara felt a hard flutter in her abdomen that might have been the baby's first kick.

II

Peter Outchinnitov's voice came fussing and storming over the telephone like a wrong number dialed three times in a row.

"Who is this Stragan? What does he think he is doing? I will not submit my plan like a petition."

"He's the head of the county planning commission," said Moss, backpedaling. "And that's the way the planning commision does things."

"It is idiotic."

Moss was cowed by Outchinnitov's unexpected wrath.

"Well, of course, it's not what we expected, but it looks like there are politics involved. Stragan makes the decisions, and once he approves the plan, it's sold."

"But this is not another subdivision. It is an organic concept, and unless it is explained properly, the man will misinterpret everything."

"Peter, it's just as important to me as it is to you. I want the master plan to be carried out just as we've discussed it. But to do that we have to abide by certain ground rules, just as we have to work with the existing water supply. And submitting the plan this way is one of the rules."

"I detest functionaries," said Outchinnitov. And Moss could feel him giving in.

"I don't think it's going to go as badly as you expect, Peter. In fact, it might work out better for us this way. Stragan is the youngest man on the commission—he'll probably be more receptive than the others to a new idea."

There was a brief silence on Outchinnitov's end of the line, followed by the sound of paper being crumpled. Another memo?

"Now, since you were going to prepare a booklet anyway, we've already got a way to explain the plan thoroughly, with pictures and everything, so that anyone could understand it. Couldn't you just include some of the things you intended to talk about in the booklet?"

"It will cost more money."

"We'll pay it."

Their conversation seemed to settle, like a flock of startled birds.

Moss turned solicitous. "How are things otherwise? Have you been getting the information we've been sending you?"

"Yes. My architects have some truly inspired concepts for houses. And you should see the topographic model!"

"I'd like to. Why don't you ship it up here for the hearing? That ought to impress them."

"Excellent idea. I'll look into it. And I think I shall have something to show you on the master plan within a week or ten days."

"Fine."

"And how are the trees?"

"The trees? Well, the blossoms are gone, but the branches are beginning to sprout leaves."

"You haven't sprayed them, I hope."

"No, not yet."

"Don't. Insecticides poison everything alive. I recommend organic gardening. May I send you some pamphlets?"

"Certainly," said Moss. "And thanks."

"Where do you think you are going with that?" Outchinnitov had started yelling at someone else even before he put the telephone down.

The birds returned, robins and sparrows, drawn from whatever distances by the first spring stirrings of the trees. They chirped and cawed in the budding branches like religionists overrunning the site of a miracle.

And close behind them came Peter Outchinnitov in a blue Italian sports car, carrying with him, in a locked attaché case within a locked suitcase, a dummy copy of the project's master plan.

"I want you," said Outchinnitov, pulling off his driving gloves, "to imagine that you are encountering this whole idea for the first time. You are a practical man, accustomed to blueprints and architects' drawings. It is your job to read, evaluate, and interpret them, and everything about the plans you read has become routine. And then, out of nowhere, you are suddenly presented with this."

He handed Moss a fat, loosely bound book with a white, leather-like cover like a bride's wedding book; and in one corner was a hand-lettered title: THE PLUM ORCHARD: The ANATOMY OF A PROMISE.

The book was thick with pasted-down photostats, and the text was merely indicated, not set in type. Some sheets of onion-skin paper, heavily corrected, were clipped to the last page.

It seemed to be mostly a sequence of pictures, beginning with an aerial photograph of the plum orchard that showed ground moisture condensing into mist among the trees, and printed in a grainy manner that made the landscape look like an illustration for the

Book of Genesis, from which a lead quotation was taken:

And the earth brought forth grass, and herb yielding seed after his kind, and the tree yielding fruit, whose seed was in itself. . . .

The next picture was the same perspective, seen more closely. And each page, in sequence, moved closer after that. A row of trees dominated one page, then a single tree, then a branch, and then a single leaf. From this intense close-up view the camera then withdrew, once again in sequence. But now among the trees there were buildings, stone-and-wood structures with the rugged texture of earth and bark. There were low, rambling houses and two-story houses whose upper level overlooked the branches. There were buildings enclosed by trees and buildings enclosing trees in individual atria. The final picture was an aerial photograph, of the same dimensions as the first, showing the completed project, acres of trees and buildings, streets that wound and swirled and curved back on themselves, rambling main drives, patches of uninterrupted grove and tiny cul-de-sacs. And each street bore the name of a variety of plum.

"Well," said Peter Outchinnitov, "what is your first impression?"

"It's magnificent," said Moss. And he picked up the copy of the text and began to read:

This bountiful nation stands on the brink of a transcendental nightmare. . . .

America, the paper said, was facing its own annihilation and would soon choke on the greedy exploitation of its own riches. Land was being mindlessly subdivided, water- and air-polluted, human, plant, and animal nature stunted and perverted. Like wastrel heirs to a great fortune, Americans were squandering their heritage in an orgy of selfishness; and future generations, reaping this shrunken and spoiled crop, would grow up in ignorance of what the country had been and, worse, of what it might have become.

The answer, the paper said at about the halfway point, lay in nature itself, in the state of balance that was intended between man and his surroundings. That there was such a balance was beyond doubt. Poisoned water poisoned man; fouled air irritated his eyes and corroded his lungs. Sunlight and fresh air healed man internally and externally; his deepest religious beliefs were linked to the changing seasons; and trees—the trees in this orchard—not only supplied man with food and shade, but, by the process of photosynthesis, they reversed his breathing, exhaling fresh, life-giving oxygen into the atmosphere.

The Plum Orchard was to be precisely that: a plum orchard, where men could live in and with nature, caring for the trees that cared for them, in harmony with nature and in balance with the earth. The streets were scaled to men's needs, not machines', and the houses were organic units where indoors and outdoors were blended, instead of living boxes. From these surroundings there would emerge a new kind of community, where respect for life and the natural order of things would become habit. Against this rock the sea of greedy self-indulgence would crash and then withdraw, leaving an example of civic conscience for the nation and the world to follow.

Immediately after this apocalyptic preface there was a detailed description of the general plan, with specific dimensions of streets, grades, and easements, a storm-drainage system, spot elevation and slope ratios, lots for homes, and sites for parks, churches, and stores. All electric and telephone lines were to be underground. No lot was to be used for other than residential purposes except where indicated in the master plan. No building could be erected on any lot until plans and materials were approved by the architectural control committee, which would investigate quality of workmanship, harmony of design with existing structures, and the appropriateness of the location with the topography of the orchard. No dwelling could be built on any lot at a cost of less than twenty thousand dollars. No building could be located on any lot nearer to the front lot line or nearer to the side street line than the lines shown on the recorded plot. Each lot would have a minimum area of one-quarter of an acre and a minimum width. And no plum tree could be removed or mutilated unless such action was approved by the local authority after examination by a licensed tree surgeon.

There were other specifications concerning noise, temporary structures, garbage and sewage disposal, water supply, sight distance, and intersections.

All these were broken down into residential-area covenants, to which each resident would have to agree before buying or building.

Five types of houses would be built, varying in price from twenty thousand dollars to fifty thousand dollars, on lots varying in size from a quarter-acre to an acre and a half. In addition to these models, anyone was free to build his own house as long as its design conformed to the existing covenants.

Land was also set aside for a shopping center without neon signs, a recreation area with a gymnasium and community center, a grade school, and a junior high school.

There were to be no back yards. Instead, the rear of each row of houses would open onto a common mall, which was actually a small plum orchard that ended at the rear of the next row of houses. And two plum trees would be left standing in front of each dwelling. The larger streets would have a divider strip of plum trees down the middle, and even the shopping-center parking lot was to have trees between the diagonal-parking lanes.

"It's more than I had ever hoped," said Moss, setting down the book. "You've carried the idea out completely. It's as if you'd worked with the land and trees themselves."

"Ah, but we did," said Outchinnitov, crossing his legs in satisfaction. "With the topographic model. We have given each tree a number and sacrificed only what was necessary. Many trees will be removed temporarily, then replanted. This will be the definitive example of contemporary community planning. I intend to make it the subject of an entire graduate course at U.C.L.A."

"Amazing," said Moss.

"Steinbrunner will take both still and motion pictures of the project as it proceeds, to be used for future study. And a sociologist from Harvard is preparing his doctor's thesis on the project as a whole. We are about to make history here, Moss, and I thank you for the opportunity."

"What can I say?"

"We will produce a dozen copies of the master plan to begin with. The printing costs, I am afraid, will be higher than I first anticipated. However, this initial per-unit cost will decrease as additional copies are printed. And I am confident they will be. If it is used for future study, like a textbook, there may be some financial return on the plan itself. To avoid resetting type, I would like you to approve the wording before I leave."

"When will that be?"

"Tomorrow. I am meeting with a man from UNESCO in New York."

"Sure," said Moss respectfully. "I'll get it back to you tomorrow morning."

"That is satisfactory," said Outchinnitov. "You can bring it to my suite. I am staying at the Fray Junípero Serra Motor Hotel. You know where that is?"

"Of course."

"One final reminder: We must observe total security with this plan. My staff is sworn to secrecy. If word about the project should leak out prematurely, it could be disastrous. I must ask you to keep this booklet with you at all times until you return it to me."

"Certainly."

"Very well then. Now, I would like you to join me in a drink of this." And he opened an expensive-looking leather satchel and took out a bottle.

"What is it?"

"Plum brandy."

No sooner had Outchinnitov left, his car scooting away through the orchard like a large, blue beetle, than Moss was on the phone to O'Malley. After some persuasion O'Malley agreed to cancel an engagement to play snooker with a pair of local Filipinos and review the master plan with Moss that evening.

Moss was eager to have O'Malley read the plan, because he was anxious for him to like it. And he watched with growing discomfort as O'Malley picked at the binding with a fingernail and squinted at the grainy photostats as though looking for something to criticize. When O'Malley closed the book, he set it on Barbara's coffee table, and Moss jumped to move it out of a water ring.

"Sorry," said O'Malley, because he felt he must say something.

"It's all right," said Moss, examining the cover of the book.

For a moment they tried to read each other, as each had read the book.

"Well?" said Moss finally.

"The dude that wrote this, is he some kind of preacher?"

"No," said Moss a bit patronizingly. "Outchinnitov's staff put it together."

"Well, it's a fine idea and really something to be proud of. I mean that, Ray."

"Thank you," said Moss, melting and brightening. "I wanted you to like it."

"It's a little . . . there's a word, but I can't think of it. The theory part of it is all there; know what I mean? What you want to do and how you plan to go about it. But the practical part of it is a little thin. What's the word?"

"I don't think that's necessarily true," Moss began.

"Utopian!" said O'Malley with a flash of recognition. And Moss felt his neck grow warm suddenly, as though he had been called a name.

"Some of the nuts and bolts are missing," said O'Malley. And he reached out and took back the onion-skin copy of the text. "A budget, for instance. Somewhere in here you ought to list what this is going to cost and who's going to pay for it."

"Like what?" said Moss, tapping his foot impatiently.

O'Malley folded several sheets of the text back with a crackling noise. "Underground utilities, for example. You don't get those just for the asking. It costs extra. Sometimes the utility companies pay part of it, and sometimes they don't. There ought to be a breakdown of that here. And the landscaping—who does that? And who pays?"

The fact that O'Malley was slouched in Moss's favorite chair and holding a glass of Moss's liquor made such criticism seem, to Moss, like a personal affront.

"We can put the utilities underground and hire a landscape architect and add the cost to the price of each lot."

"Maybe," said O'Malley. "But how *much* will it cost? There ought to be an estimate here—for your own good, Ray."

Before Moss could begin to speak, O'Malley had started again. "And another thing: how do you expect a man to build a store someplace where he can't put up a sign? How are people to know what business the man's in?"

"Only *neon* signs are prohibited."

"But there are some stores that a community needs that stay open nights. A druggist, for example. You can't hide him away in the dark behind a flock of plum trees."

"No, of course not. There'd be floodlights or something. We'll work that out later."

"Later is too late. Ray, what's wrong about this thing is that it's looked at from only one point of view. What

144

about the shopkeepers and the light-and-power people and the phone company? They've got their problems, too. You've got to be more flexible. You can't expect to have it all your own way."

Moss had waited for O'Malley to make his point. And then he shot it back at him.

"If I can't have it my way, why do it?"

"Because your way can change if it turns out to be wrong. At least, I hope so, for your sake."

They sat quietly for a while, O'Malley watching while Moss leafed through the plan again, gathering his thoughts. Then O'Malley got up to leave.

"Gerry, wouldn't you feel differently about all this if it hadn't been prepared by Outchinnitov?"

"Could be," said O'Malley, putting on his coat. "Me and him don't seem to be on the same wave length, do we?"

"What is it about him that bothers you?"

"His breath. It goes in and out."

On his way to the front door, O'Malley poked his head into the kitchen. "You can come out now, Mrs. Moss. Night shift's leavin'."

O'Malley continued out onto the porch, where moths fluttered agitatedly around a single naked light bulb. Then he stepped into the total darkness beyond and was gone.

"What was all that about?" asked Barbara, embarrassed at having been caught hiding.

The sound of O'Malley's car starting came back across the dark.

"Compromise," Moss said. "Gerry is for it. He just doesn't seem to understand that this is something you don't do by halves."

———

The master plan was printed and submitted on schedule to the county planning commission through Chairman Stragan's secretary. But the date of the hearing had to be set back two weeks while Stragan attended a Marine Reserve encampment.

When the morning of the hearing finally arrived, an odd-looking goup of men crossed the plaza to the county courthouse: Outchinnitov, who wore a navy-blue suit cut so formally that it looked like evening clothes; Steinbrunner, bearded and ascetic; the Chinese surveyor, shy and bewildered when away from his machine; Moss, gangly and drawn, as though he suffered from insomnia; and O'Malley, fat, waddling, dissipated. Drowsy bench-warmers' eyes followed them all the way into the courthouse.

O'Malley's friend met them in the lobby and began coaching everyone in loud whispers, while the blind man who ran the candy counter listened hungrily.

"He's in a good mood today; Congress didn't cut the Corps' budget."

Eager with intrigue, O'Malley's buddy talked out of the side of his mouth and wore his hat indoors; he was easily interchangeable with a race-track tout, in the manner of all local political hangers-on. He whispered noisily until a short, trim, tanned man with thinning, sand-colored hair came striding across the marble lobby, with taps on his shoes making his heels click like horses' hoofs.

"Major—over here!" called O'Malley's pal.

The other man made a turn that was something like a military facing movement and clicked over to the candy counter.

"Major Stragan, this is Mister Moss, Mister Ouch-in-touch, and my friend Gerry O'Malley." He ignored the surveyor and photographer.

Firm and authoritative, Stragan shook hands with each man. He had blue-and-white mosaic-like eyes and the tense, overgroomed bearing of a show dog.

"Gentlemen," he said in the even tone of a man accustomed to command, "let us proceed."

They marched away in twos down a narrow corridor, Moss and Stragan in the front rank.

"How much do you weigh?" said Stragan, glancing up at Moss as they walked.

"A hundred ninety."

"I could take you," said Stragan evenly.

They rounded a corner and entered a small conference room. Four fat men in almost identical blue serge suits who had been standing outside smoking put out their cigarettes and followed Stragan's group inside.

The conference table was in three sections, forming a rectangle open at one end. In the center of the rectangle was a smaller table draped with a dark green cloth over a lump—the model. A dozen places were set around the outside tables, each with a thick yellow pad of paper and a freshly sharpened pencil.

While the other men shuffled undirected to their places with a lot of nodding and smiling, Stragan strode directly to the closed end of the rectangle and ran his hand along the cross-table, checking for dust. He seated himself first, and with a lot of coughing and scraping of chairs, the others all followed.

In the manner of boys, each man had sought to sit next to a friend, so that the two facing tables confronted each other like labor and management. Three beefy businessmen looked across at Moss, O'Malley, and the

Chinese surveyor. And those two men who appeared to lead the two groups, instead of being seated at opposite poles, met at the cross-table; Stragan and Peter Outchinnitov, each of whom refused to follow anyone else, had taken seats side by side.

They made an odd pair. Outchinnitov, with his long silver hair and dark-blue suit, like an iceberg at sea, was meticulous to the point of dandyism. And Stragan, his jaw jutting as though trained for the pose, wore a creased-sleeve sportscoat and ruler-straight black knit tie with his own meticulous attention to austerity. He wore a wedding ring, yet Moss was sure he maintained the career officer's practice of sewing his own buttons and ironing his own shirts.

"Gentlemen," said Stragan in a barking, strident voice that seemed to be aimed at the table in front of him, "let us introduce ourselves." He nodded to the heavy end man at the businessmen's table, who rose awkwardly and announced himself as Cooper Overall. The man next to him, a Mister Syl Blish, remained seated. They continued around the table until Moss, at the opposite end, had been introduced.

While this was going on, a woman tiptoed in carrying a stack of white booklets—copies of the master plan, one of which she set before each man, making a wincing smile as she did so. By the time the introductions had ended, she had tiptoed out and closed the door.

"We will now take up the matter," Stragan resumed addressing the top of the table, "of the residential subdivision proposed for the land known as the Bagliassissi Ranch."

He spoke laboriously, in the manner of men who admire force.

"Before each of you is a copy of the so-called master plan, incorporating maps and photographs of the property and surroundings. I understand that we will also see a complete exhibit or model."

"That is correct," said Peter Outchinnitov.

"Very well," said Stragan as he wrote "MODEL" on his note pad. "Now . . . Gentlemen, according to the hearing program, we should begin with the introduction of any remarks or information considered necessary by the builders. So we will now hear any necessary remarks or information. If any additional remarks or information are considered necessary."

Moss looked at Peter Outchinnitov. And O'Malley looked at Moss. Stiffly, Moss rose and began to speak.

He explained that he had first come to the area as a university student and had become so impressed with the local climate and countryside that he had decided to make his home there. But a young man's first responsibility is to make something of himself (to which two of the businessmen nodded in agreement), which Moss had proceeded to do, working his way up to the position of project manager of Rancho Estates Incorporated. In this position he had acquired a good deal of experience in the construction and merchandising of subdivision homes and an understanding of home buyers' wants and needs. He had also come to the conclusion that most subdivision land was not being developed properly because builders tended to ignore the possibilities of the land itself. And he had decided that his next project would be to build homes of the type and in the area that he would choose for his own family. As a site for such a development, he had acquired some property that he had admired for years and secured the professional talents of one of the nation's outstanding architects and planners, Mister Peter Outchinnitov, to develop it.

Then, as the man across from him checked his watch, Moss abruptly sat down and stared at Peter Outchinnitov, who glanced at the Chinese surveyor.

"Wayne," he said softly, and the boy rose, walked around the far end of the table and removed the green top cloth from the model.

They all leaned forward to get a look.

The exhibit was as intricate and thorough as a model railroad. Bits of green sponge on dark-dyed matchsticks indicated the trees, set in sand darkened also to represent soil. Black streets with white sidewalks wound among the trees, with little model vehicles at intervals, as though halted in mid-journey. There were houses built of miniature siding and brick, topped by roofs of tiny cedar shakes. Around a few houses there were tiny people occupied with domestic chores, and a small American flag flew from a model pole in a model schoolyard.

While the others examined the model, smiling and nodding to one another in approval, Peter Outchinnitov rose and pushed his chair quietly up against the cross-. table.

"You see before you a complete scale model of the planned community to be called 'The Plum Orchard.' There are, as you can see, several important differences between this and any customary type of subdivision. First of all, let me make clear that this is not a futuristic forecast of a mature development. It is the way the community will look upon completion of construction. The trees are those that are on the land now, full-grown fruit-bearing plum trees, not small saplings. Each building has a southern exposure to make maximum use of sunlight. There are no utility poles, for all electric and telephone lines are buried underground. The colors and textures of the building materials used in the homes are planned to complement the tones of the earth and trees. There are no billboards of any kind, merely two stone gateposts at each entrance bearing the name of the community. Each home is designed to make maximum use of the cool shade and green, growing beauty of the trees themselves. It is, gentlemen, a completely organic community, planned to grow naturally, as a tree itself grows."

He spoke in a deep, melodic voice, each statement confirming and amplifying the one preceding it, as when an intelligent question leads to a thorough and complete reply. He spoke some words the other men had only seen written, and the strangeness of these along with his curious accented pronunciations lulled and fascinated them at the same time. They listened, quietly attentive, as the late-morning sunlight came through the windows and warmed the bare room. And when he finished, glancing at each man as he sat down, there was a satisfied silence, as though he had hauled them all to the summit of a hill.

"Are there any questions?" asked Stragan.

There was a pause on the brink of a final, intuitive approval. But the only man who could grant it chose not to.

"Since none of the other commissioners have questions," said Stragan, "I will ask a few."

From the summit a quick and sickening descent now came into view.

"Now, I believe in esthetic beauty as strongly as the next man, but . . ."

And the word was like a shove.

". . . there are practical considerations to be made in a plan like this. The question of underground utilities presents a problem."

Moss felt O'Malley look toward him.

"We'll pay the difference," said Moss.

Stragan frowned at the interruption. "As I was saying, the question of underground utilities presents a problem. The problem is one of cost, as underground utilities are expensive. Our county supervisors' approach to this problem was to enact an ordinance requiring all electric and telephone utility lines to be put above ground. Because they chose this manner of solving the problem, many new industries have chosen to locate in this area. Now . . . Though this may inconvenience some homeowners or offend some people's esthetic taste, it has worked out well for the firms that —after all—pay the lion's share of our county property taxes."

"Are there exceptions?" said Moss anxiously from the end of the table. "If we're willing to pay extra, the utility companies won't mind."

Stragan set his jaw. "There are no exceptions while I am chairman of this commission. A local ordinance is the law. If you want to change the situation, change the ordinance."

Outchinnitov, seated beside Stragan, turned to stare at him as though trying to recognize him from a block away, and as he stared, Outchinnitov's normally deep sun tan seemed to drain from his face.

"Another problem," continued Stragan, "is the question of streets. You may not be aware of the fact that we have a traffic problem—and a tough one, I'm not ashamed to admit it. The state and federal governments have spent millions to get vehicles moving efficiently from place to place along the highway, which is our main artery. The problem, in a nutshell, is through traffic—and we're constantly studying ways to get people from place to place directly. Now . . . Here we have a whole development of streets that do everything but that. Why must these streets curve and bend when the property itself is flat? Why are there only two entrances to the highway?"

Moss turned toward Outchinnitov, who still looked too appalled to answer. Then he replied himself.

"It's been laid out that way because curved streets are quieter, and they make pleasant places to walk."

"Walk?" said Stragan contemptuously. "Nobody walks these days. They drive to visit their next-door neighbors. They're all getting soft and fat like these four here." And he nodded toward his four fellow commissioners. A sheepish smile flickered on each of the four fat faces; then they cooled and grew firm, like warm, pliant candles whose flames have been blown out.

"You understand now," Stragan continued, "that I like your basic concept. It's clever. But before I can agree to issue you the necessary licenses and permits, your project must conform to the laws of this county, just like any other subdivision. So, some changes will have to be made. They seem reasonable to me. First, telephone and electric lines must be put above ground, as the county requires. Secondly, streets must be laid out in the normal grid pattern approved by the county, with through access to the highway for the connecting cross-streets. Now . . . That's all the law requires you to change. And that's all I'm asking you to change. Is that unreasonable?"

There was a perturbed tone to Stragan's last remarks, O'Malley noticed—an eagerness to get things settled. But before O'Malley could speak or make a sign, Peter Outchinnitov started talking, expelling air as though he had been holding his breath.

"You do not understand. This is a master plan for a complete, organic community. You cannot cut it up to fit a set of ordinances conceived for exactly the opposite purpose. I will not permit it to be turned into a checkerboard full of telephone poles. The other houses and businesses of this county have been built to conform to local laws, which serve as guidelines. But my master plan is based on law older than any ordinance: the law of nature."

Nature, to Harry Stragan, was where you went on weekends, preferably in the company of men, all armed, to camp out and kill game. No lights. No plumbing. And no place for women and children.

"I enjoy nature as much as the next man. But if we start disregarding local building ordinances, it'll set this country back a hundred years."

"Ah!" said Peter Outchinnitov, "you are beginning to understand."

Stragan was also as tolerant of eccentricity as the next man, but after all, there are limits. And there was something about the way this bunch dressed and talked that suggested a lack of respect for authority. Now they were challenging the law. The situation clearly called for firmness.

"Damn it, gentlemen," said Stragan, who avoided profanity unless his patience was taxed, "the law of nature isn't legal."

Peter Outchinnitov's mouth fell open with a slight sucking sound. And Moss felt an inward sigh, a distant, brittle breaking, a pang of old age, a catch in the chest, like weeping.

He liked the plan; Stragan wanted to make that clear. He felt that it had real possibilities. But there was an area in which it came in conflict with the law. And those ordinances wouldn't be on the books if there weren't good reasons for them.

Because he liked the plan so much, and only because he did, Stragan was willing to make allowances. The commission could delay voting on the question of approval or disapproval so that the necessary changes might be made and the general plan resubmitted at some future date. The other commissioners enthusiastically agreed, and Stragan declared the hearing adjourned.

Behind Stragan the commission members filed out, leaving the conference room as quiet as a city on a Sunday morning. Moss, O'Malley, Peter Outchinnitov, Steinbrunner, and the Chinese surveyor sat stunned and disorganized, like some guerrilla band that has lost not only a battle but a purpose.

"That's the first time," said O'Malley, "that I ever saw an idea get liked to death."

Part Four

Part Four

I

The first night in their new house Vyola Olinger had the dream again. She was in the city, exactly what city she wasn't sure, and it was night. She'd been to a movie, and afterwards she had joined a crowd of people on the curb to wait for a bus, standing toward the rear of the crowd, as was her habit, to avoid any pushing or shoving. The other people all looked forward, watching for the bus or talking among themselves. All of them but one. One person—one face—was turned away from the rest, staring at her. It was the face of a giant Negro with an oval-shaped, clean-shaved head like a coffee bean. He was looking directly at her, and he was grinning. Vyola tried to avoid his stare. She looked in every other direction, but every time she glanced back, there he was, grinning. Panicking, she turned and started to walk away. Heavy footsteps followed her. She entered a park and hurried down a narrow walkway with thick shrubbery all around, and the footsteps continued after her. The faster she walked, the faster they followed; the deeper she fled into the park, the darker it became all around her. She could hear panting, but she was too frightened to turn around. She was running out of breath, and there was a pain in her side. And the footsteps were drawing closer. And just when the steps and the panting breath and the hulking presence behind her drew so close that she expected to be grabbed at any moment and was clutching her purse to swing in resistance, she saw a light. A street light at the edge of the park. And a man beneath it, reading a newspaper. A white man. With energy beyond exhaustion, she ran toward him and called out with her last breath, "Help! He's after me!"

And the man, putting down his newspaper, looked at her calmly and said, "Well, I believe those people have the same rights as anybody else."

At that point Vyola always woke up.

The strange thing was that the man holding the newspaper had always been her husband. But that night it had been the man who had sold them their new home. Raymond Moss.

She was soaked with perspiration and too keyed up to sleep, and with a hateful glance at her husband, snoring peacefully in his twin bed, she took her dream book into the living room to read.

By dawn she had it figured out. Raymond Moss was going to sell homes to colored. They'd be living on the same block, singing, dancing, going to the same schools. She'd read the list of restrictive convenants they were asked to sign—and there was nothing in there about colored. So that was it. There was only one thing for them to do: move out. Sell the house and find a good all-white neighborhood. She knew what her husband would say. They couldn't afford it. Well, she had news for him. There were some things you just couldn't afford *not* to do. And yet he was right; they couldn't afford it. Not on his income. They would have to move out of this county with the nice climate and cute shops. They'd have to deny themselves everything nice. Damn him anyway. By the time he got up, she was furious at him. He was standing in the middle of the bedroom, holding up his pajama bottoms, when she rushed past him and collapsed, sobbing on her scattered bedclothes.

"Vyola, what's the matter?"

"You son of a bitch," she muttered bitterly, "Even your income is moderate!"

And after he'd failed to understand what was bothering her or to cheer her up, and she'd sent him off to the office, Vyola did her hair and her nails and put on her shopping outfit: stretch pants and spike-heeled Cossack boots. Then she walked to the project manager's office to talk to Mister Raymond Moss in person.

Vyola was a short woman who weighed thirty pounds more than she was willing to admit, but less than her stretch pants would indicate. She wore her still-blond hair pulled straight back and tied at the rear of her head in a bun, and from the expression on her face, you could tell that it hurt.

She marched right into the tract office, past the salesmen waiting around spinning webs, and sat down in the chair nearest Moss's office. Through the door she could hear him talking on the telephone, slow and sort of wistful. He never laughed, she thought. And he had such sad eyes; yet they said he was still in his thirties.

The first time he came out, he didn't even notice her. He just leaned his head out and told his secretary to dial him somebody in Los Angeles. Then he closed his office door and took the call inside. He must have talked for three-quarters of an hour. And people said *she* was gabby. Well, she'd made up her mind that she wasn't going to wait a minute longer than she had to, and just a second or two after she'd heard him say good-bye, she just opened his door and and barged right in—and caught him drinking whisky at ten o'clock in the morning. There was an open bottle, half empty, right on his desk, big as life. And a water glass in his hand with about two inches of whisky in it.

Seeing her, he didn't take his drink, but he didn't make any attempt to hide it either. He just set it on the table next to the bottle, in plain view of them both.

"Good morning, Mrs. Olinger."

His tie was loosened, and he needed a shave, and there were big black circles around his eyes.

"What can I do for you?"

He didn't even have the common decency to be ashamed, much less to offer her a chair. She had to pick up a bunch of papers and set it on the floor before she could sit down. Meanwhile, he'd put his big feet up on his desk.

Vyola held her temper, but it wasn't easy.

"Mister Moss, I'd like to ask you some questions about this community."

"Go ahead," said Moss with a heavy sigh that seemed to express a profound disinterest.

Vyola said that she had just walked from her house to the sales office and had noticed the street sign at her corner for the first time. The name of the street she lived on, she discovered, was "Tragedy." She and her husband had thought all along it was "Pageant." "Tragedy," she contended, was a horrid, gloomy name for a place to live.

Moss manipulated his feet around on his desk so that he faced her sideways, while leaning far back in his chair.

Tragedy, he explained, was a variety of plum, "purple with green inside—tastes a little like Concord grapes." Like all the other streets in the community, her street was named after a type of plum. The names of the streets were registered with the county planning

162

commission and appeared on maps. Changing the name of a street now would be very difficult.

"Oh damn!" said Vyola, disappointed. "We'll have to put it on our Christmas cards!"

Moss suggested that she wait until the rest of her block was built up and the homes occupied. Then there would be enough people to sign a petition to have the name changed. By that time, he figured, she'd be used to it.

Still dissatisfied, she leaped to the real problem.

"Mister Moss, do you sell homes to anyone?"

Moss explained that they were very selective and sold homes only to people with enough money to buy.

"Would you sell a home to colored?"

Moss said that he didn't know. No colored people had ever come out to look at one of his houses.

"None?"

"Not one."

But what if one did come out and wanted to buy. Would Moss sell him a house?

Moss didn't answer the question. Instead, he posed another question. Suppose, as had actually been the case so far, not a single colored person expressed any interest in buying. What if no Negroes wanted to move into their community?

Of course they wanted to move in, Vyola insisted. Just look at the dumpy places they lived in now, the filthy, run-down neighborhoods.

"Maybe they like those places better," said Moss. "After all, Negroes think differently than we do, don't they?"

They sure did, Vyola agreed. They had only one thing on their minds—the men especially.

Then, said Moss, how do we know what kind of place would appeal to a Negro?

Vyola frowned and bit her lip and looked distrustful and perplexed. She had the feeling that Moss was hinting at something awful that she wouldn't want to hear.

"I don't see any point," said Moss, "in excluding someone who doesn't want to live here in the first place. Do you?"

Vyola wasn't sure whether she'd got what she'd come for—he had such a sneaky way of saying things.

"Isn't it a bit early in the day for that?" Vyola looked accusingly at the whisky. It was an old habit of hers. Whenever she couldn't think of anything to say, she started talking.

"Early for most people," said Moss, "but late for me. I've been here all night, Mrs. Olinger, and I'm very tired. And I just might have several drinks before I turn in."

Vyola sniffed her disapproval. "Good day, Mister Moss."

"Good night, Mrs. Olinger."

Moss closed his eyes as she slammed the door; they ached with fatigue, and he was burning with a fever beyond the ordinary warmed-over heat of a night without sleep.

It always took about three months for them to get used to it all, new house, new address, new neighbors. For a while they were full of questions and complaints. And then it became home.

Moss told his secretary he was leaving for the day, and she seemed relieved to hear it.

When he reached home, Moss stripped to his shorts and lay on his bed, behind blinds drawn against the sunlight. He crooked a forearm over his eyes and tried to sleep, sweating, remembering that this was exactly how he had lived when he'd worked nights in the brewery. He seemed to be developing an old man's mind, mostly memory. And then the baby started to fuss and reminded him that things weren't entirely the same after all.

There had been rumors after the hearing that Peter Outchinnitov had flown into a rage and had physically destroyed his scale model of the master plan. Moss could neither confirm nor deny such suggestions. Outchinnitov had left the hearing seemingly in control of himself, bidding everyone a quiet good-bye before departing for Los Angeles. Following his instructions, Wayne, the surveyor, and Steinbrunner had remained to crate up the model. Later, it was said, in the privacy of his studio Outchinnitov had taken a fire ax off the wall and smashed the exhibit to bits, down to the last sponge-and-matchstick plum tree, while shrieking that he was "being eaten alive by snails." The source of this account, Steinbrunner, was suspect, as Outchinnitov had unceremoniously fired him shortly after his return to Southern California. But Moss had never seen the model again, and the one time it was mentioned to Outchinnitov, he suavely said that it had been "dismantled."

In the face of Outchinnitov's determined refusal to compromise his plan in any way, Moss had decided to sell the orchard. Outchinnitov promised to find him an orange grove in Southern California that they could develop into a true planned community, and Moss had just about decided to go ahead with the sale. And then he had a talk with O'Malley.

It was one of those foggy California days that admit no difference between ten o'clock in the morning and four in the afternoon. Barbara had gone to see the doctor, and Moss and O'Malley were left at home in the gray, empty weather. For several days following the hearing Moss had bided his time, trying to make a decision. And O'Malley, packed and ready to travel, had lingered, waiting to see what Moss chose to do. Time hung between them like a hammock, which they filled with business talk and let sway lazily.

Eventually O'Malley got around to asking Moss what his plans were, and Moss said that he'd had offers from other developers and that he planned to sell and get out. But when they got to talking about what Moss was going to do after that, Moss wound and weaseled until it was clear to both of them that he didn't have any first-hand knowledge of orange groves or any deep desire to live near one.

Why not stick it out, O'Malley suggested. Moss still had the trees. He could let Stragan have his phone poles and straight streets and still make a fine subdivision out of it.

Moss balked. It wouldn't be the same.

It would be better than watching someone else come in and tear everything out, O'Malley reminded him.

Suppose, O'Malley suggested, that Outchinnitov's original plan for the development had put the power poles above ground and set the streets straight. Wouldn't Moss have bought the idea?

He probably would have, Moss admitted.

Well, that was exactly what he could do now. On the other hand, what would he be left with if he sold? The orchard would be subdivided; no one could afford to farm it now. Moss would have made a defiant gesture that would be completely wasted upon a man like Stragan. And Moss, as a builder who had failed to complete his project, would be a less attractive risk to a bank or investors.

"It's not a very promising business philosophy, lad— 'If at first you don't succeed, to hell with it.' "

Moss, instead of being depressed by this pragmatic discounting of his prospects, began to feel relieved and encouraged. If he had no choice, he couldn't chose wrongly, and his only responsibility would be to make the best of things. Anything out of the ordinary that he accomplished would be looked upon as something of a miracle. Besides, O'Malley had talked him into it—so it was his responsibility, too. And with a sense of resignation and of purpose, Moss made up his mind to go ahead and make what he could out of the plum orchard.

When Barbara came home, in bloom and glowing, the vague brooding atmosphere that had followed the hearing was gone.

Eagerly anticipating an end to idleness, Moss and O'Malley had talked all afternoon, and the first thing Moss did was to sit Barbara down to listen while he enthusiastically explained their plans. She nodded politely and tried to get excited, while O'Malley just sat, studying them both.

O'Malley's tactfulness surprised her. When Raymond asked him to stay for dinner, he declined.

Along about sunset, the fog lifted and the edge of the sky caught fire. The trees and the ground and the distant hills burned with a slanting orange light until all that was left outside was a deep, charred blackness.

Moss wondered if he would be able to change it all just enough so that it could remain the same.

For several months, Moss and Barbara had been without an income, their savings draining away or evaporating like reservoir water in a drought, exposing all the frivolous and extravagant things they'd ever done like so many sandbars and mossy banks.

Now the first bank loan was due. And once the decision had been made to go ahead with the project, there was only one possibility: selling some of the highway frontage to commercial developers. If Moss chose carefully, eliminating industries, and walled the commercial enterprises off from the homes with rows of trees, the damage might be minimized. Hopefully, he called Berg and told him he was now willing to listen to any reasonable offers.

Like a farmer watching rain clouds, Moss scanned the horizon for interested parties who would take his land and give him money.

It turned out that there were only two solid prospects willing to consider paying Moss's asking price: the local representative of a nationwide chain of discount department stores, interesting in buying or building an outlet in the immediate area; and a used-car dealer named Eastman, who had just acquired a franchise to sell new Chevrolets.

At first Moss tried to goad them into bidding against each other, but when they discovered that there were only two interested parties, the bidding stopped; and Moss was forced to sell two large highway-frontage lots for less than he had expected, in order to pay the bank loan on time. These business firms had no trouble getting approval from the county planning commission, and within two weeks after the conclusion of the sale, both firms were ready and eager to break ground.

Moss's own plans, however, were not yet approved. Or resubmitted. Or even revised. Although he knew that he still needed Peter Outchinnitov's over-all plan and his designs for houses, Moss shrank from calling or writing him. And then, one morning while he was taking the first bite of his breakfast toast, Outchinnitov called him.

He had found an orange grove less than two hours from Los Angeles for Moss to buy. Moss could sell his plum orchard immediately and move to Southern California, where there were fewer Philistines in public office and less distrust of the imaginative. There they would build a truly organic community that the whole world would come to see.

Sheepishly, Moss declined; and like an artilleryman who loads a fieldpiece and braces for its concussion, he told Outchinnitov that he planned to go ahead with the plum orchard, then moved the phone away from his ear when the planner began to reply.

Outchinnitov was furious; he was so angry he forgot his accent and lapsed into insulting slang. He called Moss a fink and accused him of selling out. Worst of all, he threatened to sue. He vowed that if Moss ever tried to compromise his master plan to suit Stragan's nit-picking instructions, he would stop him. He would get an injunction; he would slap a lien on the property. He'd see to it that Moss lost his ass.

While Moss looked pleadingly at Barbara and tried to insert a word, Outchinnitov's anger mounted; it seemed to rise in his throat, choking him until he uttered strange guttural, animal-like sounds. Moss said it sounded as though there was interference somewhere along the line and hung up, shaking.

(It was at this time, according to Steinbrunner, that Outchinnitov destroyed the model of the master plan.)

For a moment Moss had a frightening vision of a net of carefully woven laws being dropped over his head while attorneys circled over his property like vultures.

"Ray, are you going to finish your breakfast?" said Barbara.

With a shout Moss ran into the bathroom.

"Aaarrgh!"

The day rose warm and clear as Moss sat on the porch and looked out at his plum trees. And when he felt he had detached himself enough from his own problems so that he could begin to comprehend Outchinnitov's state of mind, he wrote a letter:

Dear Peter:

I can't tell you how sorry I am about the unfortunate tone our telephone conversation took this morning. Let me just assure you that I still have the utmost respect for you as a person, and I understand and appreciate your position. You have every right to stick to your guns and uphold your professional standards, and I admire your commitment to the master plan. I wouldn't have requested your services in the first place if I didn't know you would believe in your work.

By the same token, I wish that you could understand my position a little more clearly. In the same way that you are committed to your plan, I am committed to my orchard. I have daydreamed about this one piece of property for years, and to see it developed by someone else would be more than I could bear. It is a "make or break" proposition with me. I have staked everything on it—my savings, my career, my own hopes and dreams. No other piece of land will do. I *must* go ahead. And to do so, I need your plans.

I promise you that the changes in the master plan will be kept to an *absolute minimum*. We will conform to local laws where necessary, while continuing our efforts to win the local authorities over to our way of thinking. You will be paid your full fee, just as if you continued supervision of the project until its completion. And your name will not be associated with the project in any way, unless you wish otherwise.

In return for this full payment and release from responsibility, I ask only that you refrain from taking legal action against me. The risks I have already taken in behalf of the plum orchard should be evidence enough of my sincere wishes to maintain the character of the orchard and the plan insofar as it is possible.

Sincerely,

Raymond Moss

Moss sent the letter that afternoon by airmail. Two days later it was returned unopened.

"The son of a bitch," said O'Malley ruefully when he saw the returned letter. "I knew he'd drag professional integrity into this. Well, Ray, I guess it's up to me."

"What do you mean?"

O'Malley's tongue was coated, as though it had been doing some deep intestinal dredging.

"He's a con, like I told you from the start. And every con man has a weakness—another con. I've been thinking about going south anyway—got some personal business to attend to. So I'll talk to this dandy and get him to forget his lawsuit."

He said all this with a grim purposefulness that left little room for disagreement. And when Moss began to speak, O'Malley cut him short. "Save it. I'm leaving in the morning." Then he went away.

Moss was certain he intended to get drunk.

O'Malley stopped by early the next morning, crumpled and bent like a used Dixie cup. He'd slept two hours in his car, hadn't washed or shaved, and felt too rotten to get out of the driver's seat. Somewhere during the night he'd bought two gallons of red wine and forty cans of ravioli, which rolled around loose in the flat storage area of the wagon, flashing tin lids and full-color labels.

O'Malley waved off all attempts at conversation. Instead, looking up at a dense, low sky, across which gray clouds rolled like switch engines, he offered only this word of parting:

"That sky looks like my stomach."

He backed his car around and sped away, ignoring bumps and gullies, his tires mauling gravel, dragging a long curtain of dust behind him through the trees.

Reluctantly, Moss agreed to let the commercial builders start grading. He heard the sounds of their machinery beginning work, but he wouldn't watch. Instead, he waited till evening and then walked down along the highway.

Surprisingly, the ground was not torn up at all. The little clumps of weeds and country grasses still grew along the aisles where they had thrived for years. The trees, however, were gone—without a single turning of the earth. Only a little hole remained to mark each trunk; a hole, a few paces, and then another hole, leading away in an empty rank or file until it stopped abruptly at the first of the surviving trees. No trunks or leaves or branches were scattered about on the ground. No tractor marks had scored the earth. It had been a clean and sudden abduction. And Moss never did find out just how they had gone about it.

Soon the cutting and filling began in earnest. Giant graders charged out onto the highway, interrupting traffic; the air had a gritty feel; and diesel machinery sent up a chorus of ripping, tearing noise that began at eight-thirty and ran until five.

Either the noise or the movement served as an eviction notice for a swarm of varmints who had been residents of the orchard. They overran the house and looked for sanctuary in the cellar or on the porch. Owls, squirrels, rabbits, field mice, a tortoise, and even a snake, who hid in the living room until he gave himself away by making a critical judgment. He hissed at TV.

The noise and the dirt and the thought of small, crawly animals hiding around the house made Barbara jumpy, and twice she thought that she had begun having contractions. Moss called the doctor each time, but the physician refused to get excited or to induce labor. It was a false alarm, he said, and sure enough, each time the symptoms went away.

Moss began getting strange telephone reports from O'Malley in Los Angeles. There had been some difficulty. O'Malley had driven out to Outchinnitov's business address, located high in the Hollywood hills.

"It's the weirdest-lookin' place I ever saw. First, there are a dozen men at work, half of 'em hammerin' and buildin', erectin' walls and layin' brick, busy as hell, puttin' up the oddest assortment of buildings in Christendom, all experimental and too small for any kind of human habitation. There's an imitation Aztec temple, a bomb shelter, a house without windows and a house that's all glass, and even a half-sized farmhouse with geese waddlin' around outside and a jackass peekin' out over a Dutch door. As I say, half the men are at work buildin' this mess. The other half are tearin' it down, carefully savin' everything, removin' the bricks one by one and cleanin' them off with cloth, even hammerin' each nail straight. No sooner does one gang complete a building, then the other starts to take it apart. The workmen are all young lads, students of his, I guess, and from the look of things, they switch from one gang to the other.

"Up back of all this, stuck right into the hillside, is Outchinnitov's studio. It's the shape and color of an egg with a window in the roof. When you get inside, there's a stream runnin' right through the building on its way down the hillside. And a big tree is growin' up through the floor and out the window in the roof. I'm sure I heard birds, too. You go inside and across a little bridge over the stream, and there's this tree, as big around as a redwood, with little ferns growing beside it. Next to the tree, right in among the ferns, is a secretary of some sort. She's got no lipstick on, just that funny rice-powder make-up and hair that hangs down to her waist. She's readin' a paperback book and sittin' at a desk that looks like it was made there, all tied together with rawhide, and when I say hello, she looks up as though I'm interruptin' something.

"I tell her the name's O'Malley, and I want to see her boss; and she says he's busy, and since I don't have an appointment, I'll have to wait. So I wait. He's got a little sunken living room there with those chairs that put your ass in a sling and bring your knees up level with your eyes and a table no more than six inches high with expensive-looking magazines stacked on it. All pictures. There's some paintings hangin' on one wall that look like they got left out in the rain. And off in one corner—except it's not a corner, it's a kind of curve—there's a crazy-lookin' thing that appears to be a bunch of old car parts and a mop and a hatrack. And there on the table, next to a stack of magazines, is a gun.

"Not an ordinary kind of gun, mind you. This one's

handmade and held together by friction tape, and there's a little label with typed instructions on the handle. It says: 'Pick me up. Point me at the corner of the room. Pull my trigger.' So I do. A little light flashes on, and I wiggle the beam around in the part of the room where this crazy-lookin' rig is. And then, all of a sudden another light goes on inside the rig itself. And it begins to move. Gears turn, wheels spin, the mop and the hatrack start to wigwag like arms. This goes on for maybe a minute. And then an American flag passes by on a track of some kind, and a mechanical hand comes out, takes hold of one of the hats on the hatrack—a derby, now that I think of it—and lifts it. Then the flag goes out of sight, the hand sets the hat back on the rack, and the machine turns itself off. God-damndest thing I've seen yet.

"So I start playing with this thing, and I find that this gun can start it and stop it as well, and I practice starting and stoppin' it in little bursts, so I can see how it works; and the time goes so fast I don't even realize how long I've been waitin' when the girl tells me Dandy Pete is ready to see me now.

"His office is way to the back of the building, and one wall of it is the hill, and I mean the hill itself—dirt, rocks, and everything, right inside; you could reach out and touch it like the wall of a room. He has no desk, just a conference table with maybe a dozen chairs set around it. It looks so ordinary it seems out of place.

"Well, Pete is all smiles at first. I guess he didn't realize why I'd come. He asks me how I am and how you are without sayin' a bad word about anybody; he just sits there in his riding outfit and plays with his mustache. He says how it was too bad about the project, that we'd come so close to doin' something really great only to fail at the last minute. And then I say to him that it was too bad that we hadn't got everything we wanted, but that it didn't look like we had failed, because we were going ahead with the project anyway.

"Then he starts to get upset. Did I come here to tell him that we planned to defy him and use his plan? If so, he'd call his lawyers then and there. No, no, no, I say; and I give him the pitch you made in your letter: changes kept to an absolute minimum, full payment for him just as though he'd seen the job through, and no connection of his name with the project. No sale.

"His mind was soured and puckered on the idea. It's just that he's so sore about it that he can't see straight. We argue back and forth, and I guess I get pretty hot under the collar, too. I tell him just because Stragan whipped him, he shouldn't take it out on you. And he blows up. He tells me to get out, and I refuse.

" 'O'Malley never leaves,' I say, 'until the sale is made.'

" 'Is that so?' he says. 'In that case, I'll have to throw you out bodily.' And he presses a lever on his squawk box and tells the girl with the hair to call in a few of the boys. And I hear voices and runnin' feet, and I make a run for it myself. I run down a hallway and into a room, and the feet and voices are comin' after me. I climb over a partition and into another room, and I hear Pete shoutin', 'Get him! Throw him out!' And Jesus, I'm scared, 'cause some of those young fellas are *big*. I run out into the hallway again, and nobody's there—they're all pokin' around in the room or climbin' over the partition. So I duck into the one room where they won't come lookin' for me—the women's can. I close the door of a stall and sit down and wait, and everytime someone comes near the door, I put my feet up so nobody will see my shoes. But no one comes in. There's just that one girl around, and she doesn't turn up all afternoon. And I wait there until they all go home."

"What happened then?" said Moss.

"Well, nothin' really. I'm still here. In fact, I'm callin' on Pete's phone. What a long-distance bill! I'll stay here tonight and be here to greet him in the morning. It's a damned interesting place—tropical fish, birds in cages—and I haven't seen half of it. There's candy and Coke machines, so I'm okay for food until I run out of change. If he tries to throw me out again tomorrow, I think I'll hide outside in that Aztec temple or the bomb shelter. There's so much buildin' up and tearin' down goin' on around here that nobody seems to know where anything belongs. Terrific place to hide. I figure I'll stay here till I get him to give in or drive him crazy; don't much care which. Well, Ray, I'll be seein' you— I'm gonna go play with that rig and the funny gun. Call you tomorrow night. Good-bye."

Afterwards Moss wondered if he should have tried to talk O'Malley into giving up. It probably wouldn't have made any difference. O'Malley was pursuing Outchinnitov with the relish of a man who has somehow isolated that part of himself he loathes.

The next evening there was no message, and Moss lost a night's sleep worrying about O'Malley prowling around in someone's building in the dark. By morning he was worn out from worry and the effort of trying to sleep. Then O'Malley called and told him that Outchinnitov had given in.

O'Malley had hung around the studio all day, his stomach growling hollowly, waiting for a chance to talk to Outchinnitov alone. The master planner had had a grueling day. There had been argument and shouting in his office; he had had his lunch sent in. And when at quitting time the others finally left, he stayed.

After dark O'Malley had slipped silently into his office. A single light burned at the far end of the conference table, where Outchinnitov slouched wearily, running his hand through his silver-white hair. O'Malley cleared his throat, and Outchinnitov looked up. When he saw O'Malley, a mildly curious look came into his eye.

"How did you get in?"

"I never left."

He looked at O'Malley, red-eyed, rumpled, unshaven, and purposeful. And the last bit of malice drained out of Outchinnitov's face, leaving only a droopy-mustached fatigue.

"All right," he said huskily, "let's talk."

And O'Malley pulled out the chair across from him and sat down.

"I really put it to him, Ray," said O'Malley with pride. "I wish you had been there. It was like he was surrounded by one man. But you know, he seemed so sick of this whole business I think he was ready to give in anyway. He just needed somebody to say the words. Hell, that's what sellin' is all about anyway, isn't it— getting you to agree to something you've already made up your mind about? He agreed to almost everything. He insisted on his right to resell the plan if he finds someone else who's interested. I told him I thought that would be okay with you."

"Of course. How about you? You sound exhausted."

"I'm as tired as a two-dollar whore. Haven't had a night's sleep in three days. Or a good meal. Or a drink —how about *that!*"

"Go get some rest."

"I'm on the wagon, Ray. If I keep busy for another

couple of weeks, I'll have it licked. Listen, I know an architect in La Jolla who's just the man to make the changes. He's good at puttin' out fires. I'd like to take our stuff on down to him and let him work on it."

"If you want to."

"I *got* to. If I stop now, it's trouble."

"What about Peter? Did he say anything about me?"

"Well, you know, Ray, he's really not such a bad fella once you get to know him. It's just that he has to spend so much of his time bickering—that's why he's such a prick. We parted friends, and he said he had no hard feelings and all that. Oh yeah"—and O'Malley laughed to himself—"he said he'd learned something from working with you: Never do business with a sentimental shark."

II

O'Malley returned with two sets of plans: one for the orchard's future and one for his own.

The first, the revised master plan, had been altered to conform exactly to Stragan's suggestions, and when it was resubmitted, the chairman of the county planning commission was delighted. It gave him just enough of a feeling of participation to make the idea his. He glowed with pride and genuine enthusiasm, and he congratulated Moss warmly, assuring him that all the necessary licenses and permits could now be granted and that construction could begin. Why, the community would even look better this way.

The second set of plans, like the first, involved a good deal of wishful thinking.

O'Malley was going to get out of the real-estate business once and for all, sit back and take life easy, and get himself into good physical condition. He had already sworn off drinking. He was going to go on a diet, and he had made an appointment for a complete physical examination at an expensive private hospital. Emotionally firmed by his own resolve, O'Malley turned himself over to the doctors.

They found him to be every bit as healthy as he looked. That is, he was half dead. His liver was enlarged to nearly twice its normal size, and his chest X rays revealed a spot on his right lung. The doctors urged exploratory surgery, and O'Malley being already in the hospital and under their care, there was no getting out of it. And when they cut him open, they found an ulcerated growth the approximate size of a Polish sausage in the bottom of his left lung. They removed the growth, leaving O'Malley suddenly weakened, as though the cutting had hurt him more than the disease, and with a small but constant cough, as though there was something feathery caught in his throat that he could not clear. Only time would tell if the malignancy would spread. But the cough remained.

When Moss told Barbara he was bringing O'Malley home, she turned pale with shock. *That* man? In *her* house? There must be some other place, some other people to look after him.

Moss was adamant. "We're the people he stayed here to help. I'd have gone under without him."

"But he isn't a charity case, Ray. He has plenty of money, and there are convalescent homes for people just like that."

Moss reddened, blood boiling up into his face.

"He doesn't *need* that kind of home. He needs ours! He'd do the same for me—or for you, for that matter."

Angry as Barbara was, she had to admit that it was true that O'Malley would indeed care for her if she were sick; that he had never returned her open unfriendliness; and that, as Raymond said, they both owed him kindness.

"All right," Barbara agreed. "We'll try it. But if he embarrasses or humiliates me, he'll have to leave. Or I will."

Two days later, they half carried him up the front steps, Moss supporting one weak arm and Barbara the other. O'Malley looked white and strangely old and frail. There was an odor of sickness about him, and his battered brown fedora kept slipping down over his eyes.

They helped him inside and eased him down in a living-room chair. And soon as he was seated, he started coughing. His face turned crimson and he gasped for air; Barbara ran to get a glass of water.

When she came back, he'd stopped. And after he emptied the glass thirstily, he looked up at her with pale, watery eyes and said:

"I'd like to kiss you till your ears flew off."

He was so pathetic, so wasted, that his words carried no threat, just a joke. And for the first time, Barbara was touched by him.

In the afternoons, he sat on the porch and coughed. And in the evenings, he sat in the living room and coughed. He neither smoked nor drank, but he talked a lot, often telling jokes. In the mornings he seemed particularly weak and wasted, and Moss or Barbara would often have to help him out of bed.

The fact of his illness weighed heavily on O'Malley. Small things—putting on a shoe or crossing a room—suddenly required great effort. And he was more dependent on other people than he had ever thought acceptable for a man. Here was Barbara, knocked up as it was, having to move about the house and care for him, while Moss, trying to get a whole residential community under way, had an old geezer's health on his mind. He'd get up and leave if only he didn't feel so goddamn weak. Mostly, he sat in his gaudy bathrobe and waited, watching.

Grimly, Moss threw himself into his job, taking refuge in routine. He applied to the Federal Housing Administration for a commitment to insure a mortgage loan on the development. After the property was inspected by a government land planner and subdivision valuator, and the FHA had reviewed Moss's revised general plan and the individual home designs, a firm commitment was granted; and Moss arranged a loan from a title insurance company that gave him the working capital he needed to begin construction.

Like a mechanized army, the construction crews then fell upon the orchard. They bulldozed down trees and cut them up with chain saws. Doughnut-tired graders rolled back and forth over the rich topsoil until it was packed hard. They sent up a racket that drove the last bit of quiet out from under the last plum tree and filled the sky with a fine brownish powder that left a dull coat on every leaf.

And when the grading machinery left, the building machinery arrived: air compressors, lumber carriers, trenching machines, jackhammers, cement mixers, all roaring and chattering away every working day, so that walking through the development to inspect the construction work, you simply passed from noise to noise.

In this great, throbbing din human voices grew hoarse and distorted as workmen shouted and whistled instructions and warnings to one another; and the few frightened, dusty birds who clung to what life remained among the still-standing trees flew frantically from perch to perch, screeching.

At nightfall the tumult ceased, leaving a desolate and peaceless quiet, a lull in a storm. Surveying it, Moss assured himself the construction would eventually be completed and everything would return to normal. The problem was, what would normal then be like?

O'Malley was now having seizures of soft coughing that lasted far into the night, and he could not speak without clearing his throat. Moss and Barbara tried not to listen and heard all the more clearly. While the incessant discomfort lasted, they talked and read and watched television or listened to music and avoided each other's eyes.

He never complained, Barbara noticed, and he never felt sorry for himself. Not once.

To Moss's astonishment, almost every construction cost was turning out to be higher in the new development than it had been in the old one. Not only were workmen's wages higher, but the same jobs seemed to take longer. When Moss complained to the contractor about the slow progress of the building, that touchy man simply passed the blame along to the building-trades unions and material suppliers. Reese talked of jurisdictional disputes and hinted vaguely at a strike, and he said the subcontractors were crooks. All of which gave little ease to Moss.

With each day adding up to a substantial loss, Moss began to feel an urgent need to get some sort of regular income—not enough to balance his building costs, but some amount coming in every week or month to offset one of his regular expenses so that he might cancel it out of his debt and off his mind.

The best offer came from a religious group that wanted to build a community church on the present site of the storage shed, set back behind some trees and connected to the highway by an access road. They seemed amiable to the point of complete harmlessness. They were willing to sign a ninety-nine-year lease and make monthly payments on it, and they offered to leave the trees standing around the church itself and down the center of the road leading to it. Moss had Berg draw up a lease, and it was signed. Only later, when the shed had been demolished and the church, an alarmingly modern structure with a spire that resembled a space ship, had been partially completed, did the county planning commission notify Moss that trees were not permitted in the middle of county streets and more plum trees would have to go. Stragan again.

When O'Malley saw the simple silver cross on top of the church spire, he propped himself up in bed on his elbows to get a better look. From the eaves, panels of blue plastic swooped upwards toward a peak, just below the cross. O'Malley took a deep, wheezy breath and rasped one comment to Barbara before he was seized with a fit of red-faced coughing that lasted for twenty minutes.

What he said was, "God is kicks."

With infuriating slowness the first houses aged to completion. There were delays and wrangling over the cedar-shake roofing, and the lawns weren't even planted, but those first houses were built to Peter Outchinnitov's specifications. With the patios and atria and the full-grown plum trees just beyond each back door, they made you feel as though you were indoors and outdoors at the same time. They belonged on that land.

Moss whispered a wish for good weather and set about staffing up with sales personnel. He had once planned to hire Russ and possibly Buddy away from Pasquinelli, but those earlier associates of his had now become too rich and too involved with their own business interests to consider moving. Moss had to turn to local talent instead.

They came to him through the gossipy tips and leads of the real-estate fraternity: experienced salesmen, dissatisfied with their jobs; suburban office workers, fed up with commuting; failed car, door-to-door, and appliance salesmen; raw youngsters; drunks and drifters. Moss preferred experience but tried to keep his mind open for potential, and in the end hired three salesmen, all licensed, seasoned real-estate people. He wasn't taking chances on anyone like himself.

And when the directional signs went up along the highway (a concession to marketing reality that did indeed draw prospects), the people came; and the houses began to sell immediately. Had more units been completed, they would have sold, too. An encouraging sign. Moss was starting at a point it had taken two years to reach with the other development. There was a real market for these houses, a genuine desire on the part of people to own them. And he decided it would be wise to play hard to get.

He instructed his salesmen to act skeptical toward their prospects, inspecting them as they inspected the houses, advising the customers to consult with one another and visit the development several times before deciding to buy. This treatment made the houses seem even more desirable, and the sale of finished houses, lots, and even incompleted frames rapidly and steadily increased. Only the continuing building delays were limiting the sales figure.

Moss did no selling himself. He was confined to administrative chores, because the decisions involving law or money were ones only he could make. Hating detail, he wallowed in it, and on most days his conversations consisted mostly of haggling. He came to the sales office early, and he stayed late. And he began keeping a bottle of whisky and a tumbler in his desk drawer.

And then one morning O'Malley could not get up.

He lay in bed waiting for strength that never came. He couldn't prop himself up in bed, and when Moss lifted him into a sitting position, he couldn't hold it. His eyes bulged and he gasped, and Moss and Barbara eased him down until he was flat on his back, staring with huge eyes at the ceiling.

A nervous doctor came and sent for an ambulance to take him back to the hospital, and O'Malley apologized for the trouble he'd caused, as if he knew he wouldn't be coming back. The attendants eased him onto a stretcher like a worn lump of soap, all white and encrusted with hair. He looked up at Moss standing beside him with his suitcase, and handed him a wrinkled piece of paper. The name Carolyn and a phone number were written on it in pencil.

"Call her," he gasped. "She's my wife."

And as they carried him out the front door, Barbara, in her nightgown and maternity robe, bent over him, her hair falling into his face, and kissed him warmly on the mouth. Surprised, O'Malley looked at her, blinked and smiled; then they took him away to the hospital.

O'Malley had never talked or acted married. He had always seemed to belong only to himself. They must have been separated, at least.

But when Moss called long distance to Pacific Palisades, the voice on the telephone sounded young and vulnerable. And when he told her that it looked like cancer, she went to pieces, overwhelmed by pity and loss and life unrealized; and Moss felt cruel and helpless at the same time. She said she was going to come to the hospital and see him, and Moss assured her there would be plenty of room at their home for her to stay.

She arrived the next morning, a small, pretty, bird-like woman with a tight, pinched mouth and furtive eyes, who seemed to be searching for someone to take care of her. She referred to O'Malley as "Gerald" and asked nervous, fretting questions not only about his health but also about his business activities and his income.

Carolyn O'Malley stayed with Moss and Barbara only one night. When she went to the hospital the following morning to see her husband, she collapsed from nervousness and had to be kept there herself under sedation.

They removed O'Malley's diseased lung, and with that the last bit of drinker's color faded out of his face. Propped up in bed, his wasted body barely denting the pillows, he sat with Moss and Barbara, speaking only sparingly because the effort made him cough until his eyes watered.

"How long?" he whispered to Barbara, and began coughing softly.

"Six weeks," she said, inadvertently touching her swollen stomach. And O'Malley's eyes fell where her hand did, imploring the infant to hurry.

When O'Malley's wife recovered, she took a motel room near the hospital so she could come and visit Gerald every day. She talked and wept and carried on, while O'Malley watched her appreciatively. She reassured him. He was now convinced that he had done the right thing by arranging a legal separation years before.

And as he watched O'Malley lying in his bed in painful waiting or being wheeled in and out of surgery, Moss wondered if it might not have been better for him to burn up the remainder of his life the way he had consumed most of it, to simply keel over some night off a bar stool or to choke on laughter or to have a heart attack while in the act of sexual intercourse. Instead, the doctors had knocked O'Malley down and cut him up just about the same way graders remove a plum tree.

Pressed by the demand for houses, Moss urged Reese to get the units completed faster, with unhappy results. Words were passed beyond apology, and Moss fired the man, only to decide that he needed him. Moss then persuaded Reese to continue, promising a bonus. And then there was another, bitterly final argument; and the contractor quit.

Just when Moss needed houses most, construction ceased. In desperation, he agreed to allow another builder, a man named Horner, with riddled, irregular teeth that looked like lace hung in his mouth, to build houses in the orchard. Horner built in the same price range as Moss but of cheaper materials. He had his own models, standard ranch-style dwellings that looked nothing like Outchinnitovs' more rustic designs, but they could be built quickly, and they sold as soon as they were completed. Just to make sure no one was mistaken about who was building what, Moss's new associate put up black-and-yellow "Horner Homes" flags along the highway and in front of every house he built.

Increased pressure was also brought to bear upon Moss by those people who bought individual lots for homesites; they wanted him to do away with the architectural control committee, which was, in effect, Moss himself reviewing home builders' plans and specifications and insisting on minimum-quality materials and workmanship. Since he himself was now permitting houses of cheaper materials to be built in the orchard commercially, Moss realized he couldn't deny permission for individual houses to be built the same way. So he agreed to let site buyers build whatever met the approval of the county planning commission. And the county planning commission never disapproved anything because it was cheap or ugly.

As his orchard was remade, his friend O'Malley wasted, dying visibly as a flower dies, parts of him shriveling daily until he no longer resembled even his own memories. Shrunken and frail, he lingered in the cloying hospital atmosphere like a flower in a vase, uprooted and doomed, until he gasped his last tormented breath and passed away without a word.

And though Moss had expected it and had watched the life drain painfully from O'Malley a little at a time, his death both shocked and wounded him. Something went out of Moss's own life with his friend, an open, unguarded way of facing the world and of being able to say what he felt to someone he knew would do the same. He would bury this part of himself with O'Malley, and he mourned his passing for selfish reasons, in the most honest sort of lament.

We die with our friends, in pieces.

Moss returned to his work, and the full ghastliness of what he was doing and what he had become struck him like an insult. Around his sales office, the development stretched away, half trees, half houses. Shiny cars moved crosswise from block to block; black wires zigzagged back and forth above the streets. In the distance the surface of the nearest hill was scraped away unevenly, like a bad haircut. Even the rain that had fallen soft and sweet on the leaves and on the earth now gave off a sour stench as it splashed on asphalt and cement.

And when, within that same month, Barbara's turn came, and Moss drove her to the same hospital and took up the vigil for birth as he had for death, he was overcome by a deep, brooding consciousness entirely apart from the cliché anxieties of fatherhood. Silent and dazed, he waited, rudely ignoring the routinely offered solace of the nurses and interns until they made pained faces at one another and left him alone. And for one moment, one breath of utter quiet from the delivery room, he was convinced that he had lost them all in a single fearful season of reckoning.

And then it was over. Barbara was wheeled out on a hospital gurney with a red, squalling infant beside her. And Moss took her hand and strolled alongside the rolling gurney. While the doctors and nurses complimented themselves on the ease of the delivery, and the baby made its urgent, hungry clamor, Moss looked into his wife's eyes. And saw the same fierce mixture of terror and relief he felt himself.

Slowly sleep relaxed its coils, and Moss awoke, limp and bewildered. For a moment he tried to remember something he'd wanted to tell O'Malley, as though O'Malley were still alive. And then the baby cried, and bit by bit his life came back to him: the death, the birth, the frustrated plan—all the way to Vyola Olinger.

He heard Barbara talking to the baby, and he went into the kitchen. She was changing a diaper, and the tiny face, a doll version of her own, was looking up, animated with glee, while a fat, tiny hand grabbed at Barbara's glasses.

She handled the baby with easy competence; together they were agile, even graceful, as though Barbara had been destined to be part of some sort of acrobatic team and had only been waiting for the right partner.

Moss touched his daughter's hand, and her face turned toward him and went blank. He made a face at her and conciliatory cooing noises. And the child turned red and began to cry. Barbara pinned on the diaper, picked the baby up and patted her, and began pacing the room. When Moss left the kitchen, the crying stopped.

Moss washed and shaved and avoided looking at his own eyes. He was in the bedroom putting on his socks when she came in.

"You're still a stranger to her, Ray. She doesn't see you much."

"Um."

"She'll change. Girls always like their fathers."

Moss concentrated on tying his shoes.

"Are you going back to work? It's nearly five."

"I'm going down to talk to that car dealer. Somebody ought to give him hell."

He picked up a sports coat by the collar and slipped into it as he walked toward the door. Barbara followed him.

"I'll call you if I can't make it for dinner."

She touched his arm and then embraced him and offered her face to his. He kissed her and left.

The Chevy dealership sprawled along the highway for a full block. At first the dealer had contended to Moss that he needed the extra land paved for parking; but once the asphalt was down, he turned the space surrounding his showroom into a giant display area with two square acres of new and used cars, pickups, trailers, a boat, and even an airplane spreading out from an illuminated marquee that read: WE'RE RED HOT AND ROLLING.

Moss cornered the dealer in the middle of his stock and began berating him, accusing him of betraying his word and his community, deploring his venal vulgarity.

The dealer, a compact man named Eastman, with black hair that curled tightly around his head and wide, alarmed eyes, listened for several minutes and then returned in kind. Soon they were shouting at one another beneath a flapping cloth banner that identified "Friendship Chevrolet."

Knowing he would gain nothing, Moss persisted, saying aloud the things to Eastman that he had been telling himself, until, realizing in frustration the impossibility of insulting a car salesman, he got it all out, and the dealer began trying to smooth things over.

As Eastman talked, his voice growing soft and conciliatory, Moss's attention wandered over the dealer's shoulder to the highway, where a large black hearse was slowing for an intersection stop light. There were kids in it and surfboards sticking out the back, and it sounded more like a boat than a car. And as it pulled to a stop directly even with him, Moss's eyes met those of a boy in the front seat by the window, a blond youngster with a sweatshirt cut off ragged at the elbows. Something about the kid reminded Moss of himself at a certain age. And the youngster looked back at Moss with the same sudden sense of recognition. As Eastman talked on, unheard, the blond kid reached out of the car and spread his arms as though to enclose everything in his field of vision and shouted at the top of his voice, "Ugly! Ugly!"

Eastman stopped talking and turned; the light changed, and the hearse lumbered noisily away.

Sourly the dealer turned back to Moss. "Kids," he said disgustedly. "What do they know?"

I've saved some trees, Moss said to himself. Whatever else I have become, I've saved some trees.

III

Spring came early that year and ripened quickly into an insistent summer of mornings that heated up instantly and afternoons that were baked until done. In the evenings, the earth gave off acquired warmth like a heating stone, and darkness came with a slow, respectful tread.

The first week of hot weather made the plum trees burst with fragrant white blossoms so thick that the trees that lined the streets or stretched away behind the houses merged into snowy blurs that softened every angle and shadow. Round a corner, and you stepped into a post card. Even in the deepest construction scars a cover of weeds, grass, and wild flowers began to grow.

Stimulated by seeing and feeling their community come alive, a few of the new homeowners trimmed off flowering boughs and used them for indoor decor; but after the first weekend, when carloads of sight-seers rolled slowly past the houses admiring the blossoms, the cutting stopped. The trees had become a matter of civic pride. And before long the display of a few freshly cut plum blossoms in a dinner-table centerpiece was certain to get a hostess a stern conservationist lecture from at least one of her guests.

As the bright, dry heat persisted, the blossoms wilted and fell. And when the trees turned green and leafy, most people lost interest in them, because any kind of tree did that.

Despite his business pressures, Moss still found time to concern himself with his trees; to him, real estate was an avocation. During the winter, he had pruned the branches himself, removing the dead wood to maintain ventilation and shape the trees. He kept a regular watch for the disease and pest signs described in the manuals he ordered regularly from the Department of Agriculture. And as he watched the trees blossom with health, a little of his old assurance began to bud and bloom.

His first plum crop, the year before, had been a disappointment. The trees had started bearing in late May, and the different varieties ripened successively until mid-August. Because Moss had taken Peter Outchinnitov's advice and avoided insecticides, more than a third of the plums were flawed, tinged with brown rot or preyed upon by tiny borers. This year, anticipating trouble, he had compromised a bit and treated the plum trees with a simple but effective sulfur spray.

To harvest his first fruits, he had used *braceros,* agricultural workers brought in from Mexico by the state and sent to Moss only when they could be spared elsewhere. He rented cots and billeted them in his partially completed houses, whose sliding doors, elaborate plumbing, and planned lighting were sources of endless amusement to the rural Mexicans. They worked the switches and handles so often that they literally wore some of them out. In the fields, they went about their work with a proud, quiet competence, taking the fruit from the trees by hand and placing it in baskets, standing on light ladders to reach the plums on the tall branches. Only at night, surrounded by the threatening darkness of a strange country, did they give in to homesickness and loneliness; they sang, got drunk, prayed, and argued, and filled the orchard with the melancholy sounds of an exile community. They worked a few days for Moss, were taken away in yellow school buses, and were brought back weeks later to work a few days more: small, dark men in work clothes and straw western hats identical as uniforms; men to whom everything was foreign but the earth and trees. When they left for the last time, it was without a backward look at the stacked field lugs, the tidy aisles, the cleanly picked branches, or the lone man who stood in their shade, waving.

It was more than the end of a season; on December 31, the state's agreement with the Government of Mexico for the importation of agricultural labor expired.

When the blossoms fell, Moss decided to have the earth around the trees Rototilled, and he had to bring a farmer in from nearly twenty miles away to do the job. With the passing of the orchards, agricultural machinery and people who knew how to operate it were scarcely available. And when the man Moss had hired chugged his tractor among the trees, turning over the soil, a curious crowd of neighborhood youngsters followed him, shouting and waving and tossing dirt clods at one another.

Moss had sold his first plums to a commerical packing plant, a branch of a huge corporation whose basic business was the manufacture of bowling equipment. It was the county's sole remaining packer, and operated largely on the energy and enthusiasm of its manager, a recent business-school graduate named Bobby Blythe. He was a bright, immensely likable young man with an alert, outthrust face that life hadn't been able to etch a line on. He avoided drink and women and threw all his energies into his job, wrestling lugs of fruit around on the loading dock, operating the forklift truck, riding out to the fields with his drivers for a firsthand look at the harvest. He hustled. By packing every available variety of deciduous fruit—pears, peaches, cherries, plums, and apricots—he kept the plant operating at capacity, three production lines, all summer long.

The parent organization noticed him. Not only had he made the plant operate at a profit; his requests for new equipment, various extra sizes of sorting machinery and packages, had convinced them of the unprofitable future of such an operation in less youthful and ambitious hands. And when the last harvest was safely in, they auctioned off all the equipment, sold the land and buildings, and quit the fruit-packing business while they were ahead.

Bobby came to say good-bye to Moss before he left. He assured him that things were still looking good; the home office had transferred him to a paint company in St. Louis with a promotion and a raise in pay. He shook Moss's hand warmly and told him that the packing house was already being renovated and would be re-opened in the near future as an antique store to be called the Old Red Barn. Helplessly, Moss wished him well.

The warm weather gave home sales an added boost, and before summer Moss had paid his last installment to the bank and was realizing a profit on every house. A large part of his job was now a kind of counseling, responding to the minor complaints of homeowners about sticky doors and windows and unreliable water heaters. Quite often, women left alone for the day would walk down to the sales office just to talk, and Moss insisted that they be treated courteously and that fresh coffee always be ready for them. Unlike most real-estate men, he understood that satisfied homeowners were his best sales force and were not to be ignored once they had taken occupancy. He catered to them and heard out their complaints, although he disliked doing it.

And as the sun bleached one day pale as the last, and the weekend crowds increased, and the streets rang with the shouts of children playing outdoors in the long, light evenings, life began to stir again deep within the plum trees. Grafted and bred not for beauty but for yield, they responded to the continuing warmth like dough and yeast set in an oven. Earlier than Moss expected, the first varieties of hard, green fruit appeared and began to ripen quickly in the constant sunlight. The sulfur spray had worked remarkably well; nothing stunted about this crop. As the fruit swelled in size and acquired its true color, the homeowners began to notice their surroundings again.

The children, of course, discovered the plums first and sampled them prematurely; several cases of severe stomach-ache and diarrhea served as an effective warning to the impulsive.

The plums grew out in clusters, big as hen's eggs; and the branches bent with their weight.

Eagerly, the homeowners anticipated their crop. Men squatted on their haunches, sifting soil or doodling with sticks, ruminating. They debated the effects of weather on the fruit; rising, knee joints cracking, they took to walking among the trees and bending down the low branches to have a look at how things were progressing. It was very satisfying. A man could endure the routine of a job or a tyrannical boss a little more easily knowing that, if nothing else, his plums were growing bigger and riper.

The women talked about putting up preserves, though few knew how. Some hunted up old recipes for dishes like plum kuchen and plum cream pie, and traded and discussed kitchen hints in the supermarket and around the tract sales office. Vyola Olinger had so many requests for her plum compote, made with wine syrup and lemon slices and once a specialty of her mother's, that she had to run off mimeographed copies.

Like primitive people, they watched the fruit grow and ripen, feeling the mystery of the earth through its natural cycle. It was as though the plums were filling up with sun itself.

Soon the first plums matured—plump, juicy Santa Rosas with tart red skin and sweet yellow flesh, each bite a mingling of contrasting flavors characteristic of no other fruit.

The people handled them with care, almost reverential in their feelings of closeness to the primary source of food. Neighbors chatted and compared specimens as they met in the shade of the communal trees. And people who had not tasted fresh plums since childhood discovered the sugary-astringent flavor all over again.

Soon, no home was without its bowl of ripe, fresh-picked plums, usually set upon the dinner table for dessert. Someone learned that the newly opened antique store, the Old Red Barn, was selling the little tin-rimmed veneer baskets that you used to buy plums in at neighborhood groceries, and the whole supply was snapped up in two days. Lined with purple tissue and filled with fruit, they made handsome gifts.

Those people who owned long ladders found them repeatedly in demand from neighbors who wanted to reach the plums remaining higher in the trees. No one, it was widely said, had ever bought fresh fruit that tasted better; and each homeowner felt rich in a way that he never had before, as if he possessed part of the earth itself.

And when the excitement and novelty of the first fresh plums began to fade a little, and a few children began peevishly yearning for a return to ice cream for dessert, the women of the community enthusiastically began exercising their kitchen expertise.

Someone discovered that by sticking a fork in a plum and holding it in boiling water until the skin cracked, you could peel it like a tomato. With the skin gone, only sweet flesh remained, to be sliced and flavored and served over cake and ice cream. In effect, this meant that the plums now came in two flavors: sweet and sweet-tart. These sweet plums were also served in salads, simmered into sauce, and finally made into jelly and jam.

The deep community pride and individual enthusiasm that the property owners felt for their crop lasted for some time. In fact, it was several weeks before the first few residents were willing to admit cautiously to one another that plums could become tiresome or even a nuisance. Because the trees, once they had begun to yield, would not stop.

No one had had any conception of the amount of fruit a single mature plum tree, pruned to permit maximum exposure to fresh air and sunlight, properly sprayed, and baked by solid weeks of blast-furnace heat could bear. Not even Moss. He had kept no records of his previous crop, for that was exactly the sort of detail work he had turned to the trees to escape. And, as his houses were rapidly occupied, he had convinced himself that the *braceros* and the packing plant had been nothing more than intermediaries between the fruit and its market. This year, both plums and people were here.

Some families had picked fruit only as they used it, while others filled boxes and baskets, intending to hoard the plums when the supply ran out. As the trees continued to yield, and midsummer plums, Tragedys, Wicksons, and Eldorados followed hard upon the earlier Santa Rosas, the families who had hoarded plums reached surfeit. And soon even those people who picked only what they consumed had more plums than they could eat or use for cooking.

Sacks and crates filled up with extra plums, and jars of plum preserves deepened rank by rank inside kitchen cupboards. There was heavy exchanging of plum pies and plum cakes for a while, until most women decided it was hardly worth the work when they got back as many plums as they were able to give away. Children were urged to take extra plums at meals or to fill their pockets with them for friends when going out to play, but all this was not enough. The heat persisted, and the trees continued to yield.

Distant relatives and friends began receiving invitations to drop by for visits, only to be sent home bewilderedly loaded with fresh fruit or jars of preserves. On a Sunday afternoon, for example, you might see an out-of-towner leaving someone's house carrying a lug of plums as the families exchanged good-byes. And if he glanced next door, the man with the plums might see another visitor like himself, carrying the same sort of box and leaving his friends' house at exactly the same hour.

The decline in the value of plums was sudden and irreversible. Gathering momentum, it grew toward panic.

Under pressure from Moss, the community supermarket filled several bins with fresh plums, red ones, green ones, purple. They made a handsome display, perfectly symmetrical because it remained untouched. When the plums began to spoil, the manager put them in the freezer, keeping them as evidence to Moss why the store could not afford to stock any more local fruit.

One enterprising group of youngsters on Becky Smith Lane attempted to make a business out of disposing of the plums by setting up sidewalk fruit stands made of card tables and old packing cases. For half a morning the first stand did a fair business; but soon so many imitators were clamoring for trade and noisily cutting prices that they drove off any passers-by who might possibly have been interested. To buy from one child was to suffer the abuse of all the others. By midafternoon, the fruit was soft from sunlight and bruised by handling, while the game of playing store had turned to tedium. The children squirmed in sullen disappointment. With no customers to yell at, they yelled at one another, taunting and teasing until one boy, a bit worse-tempered than the others, picked out one of his soggiest plums and winged it at a little girl across the street, striking her back of the ear and causing her to cry. Instantly a second plum vendor returned fire, and the whole block suddenly erupted in exchanged volleys of discarded fruit, shouts, crying, and laughter. The fighting did not cease until the last bit of produce had been reduced to a soggy mass, impossible to throw. To a child, the young entrepreneurs were soiled and disheveled; half of them were in tears. All along the block the lawns and sidewalks were littered with fruit. And the black asphalt was flecked with yellow smudges that made car tires spin.

The property owners along the street were indignant at the damage, but since the children who had caused it were their own, the blame was never fixed; and no claims were ever made. The fathers merely grumbled and cleaned up the mess.

The heat continued; the sky was weather-beaten white, and still the trees bore fruit. Some overloaded branches broke, and Moss had to brace many of the others with long stakes. The plums could not be eaten or sold or given away, and the fruit grew and ripened until it fell upon the ground and began to rot, giving off a sweet, decaying stench.

Those people who insisted on keeping their property picked up found that if they gathered the loose fruit and set it out with their garbage, the paper and bottles and cans would be removed and the plums left behind. And a box of decaying plums in the garbage was even more unpleasant than loose fruit on the ground outside.

Responding to the homeowners' complaints, Moss telephoned the scavengers' association, not once but several times, and tried to explain the problem to a woman who had difficulty with English. There were plums, understand? *Si, si.* They were being set out with the garbage, and though the rest of the garbage was being taken away, the plums were not. *Si.* Would she see that the plums were picked up next time? *Si, si.*

But nothing was ever done.

On the morning of a Monday scheduled for garbage pickup, Moss arose earlier than usual and sat on his porch in his bathrobe, waiting in ambush for the gar-

203

bage men. He heard the grinding noise of their truck and the clanking of cans and bottles. And when he looked out around the Monument, he saw a blunt, familiar figure out at the curb, sifting through the garbage pails and boxes, separating plums from paper, cans, and bottles.

"Bagliassissi!"

"Gnasheet."

Moss crossed the front yard, his bare, hairy legs trotting awkwardly beneath the skirts of his flowery silk bathrobe. Bagliassissi watched him with sweaty, denimed contempt.

"What's going on here?" said Moss, trying to sound like a cop. "Why aren't you taking these plums?"

Bagliassissi pulled a red bandanna out of his back pocket and mopped his face.

"Eesa produce. We no haul. Scavenge regulation."

"For god's sake, this is an emergency! The place is overrun with the stuff . . . there's no place to market it. People are throwing it away. It's waste . . . garbage!"

The old man picked a single plum out of Moss's garbage and held it up in his grimy leather glove. The plum was speckled with bits of eggshell and coffee grounds.

"Ees what *you* make it."

Gently he wiped the plum clean with his bandanna. The yellow garbage truck lumbered up next to them.

"That's beside the point," said Moss, remembering that his was a trained legal mind. "This is a licensed public service. You can't refuse to perform your duty."

Bagliassissi shouldered his trash sack, now filled with acceptable garbage.

"Ees my duty."

He pointed one leather finger down at the rejected plums.

"Ees a not."

Then his whole body clenched fiercely.

"You fuck up my orchard. You no fuck up my job."

Turning, he stormed away, swung the sack off his shoulder as if it were paper, and dumped its contents into the bin at the rear of the truck. He hung the sack on the truck's side, stepped up on the running board and grabbed the handrail. Looking down at the plum still in his hand, he sighed softly.

"Gnasheet."

And as the truck pulled away, he lobbed the plum back toward Moss, underhand. It bounced a couple of times, rolled into the uncut grass and stopped.

At that moment, it occurred to Moss what an utter failure he would have been as an attorney. Never in his life, not once, had he really won an argument.

The homeowners managed to dispose of some of the surplus plums. They dug holes in the earth around the trees and buried the fruit, or they hauled it miles away by car and dumped it; but the longer the fruit ripened and fell, the more effort these measures required.

With people leaving for summer vacations, the cleaning-up fell far behind. Untended aisles filled up with decomposing fruit, and the job of hauling away the excess became a kind of civic martyrdom few people were willing to endure.

The plums, ignored, shriveled on the trees, fell, and became leaky or cracked with decay. And insects came to dispose of the remains. First, there were ants, tidy and methodical, that spilled around the trees in black, syrupy lines. Then yellow jackets that hovered menacingly or perched, throbbing, on the wasted fruit. And lastly, fruit flies, tiny, slow-flying creatures that floated on the wind like cinders but seemed to take possession of the air as though you breathed them in and out. Too small to swat, they passed through screens into the houses, where people were soon forced to live in pungent clouds of insecticide.

All these pests the property owners endured with some degree of patience. It was fear of an even worse invasion that brought everything to a boil: rats.

Someone saw, or thought he saw, a large, gray rodent-like animal rooting through some plums that were lying on the ground. It might have been a squirrel; there had always been squirrels, shy creatures with bushy tails, in the trees. But whoever saw this latest animal called it a rat, and, rightly or wrongly, the word spread through the community like the clanging of a fire bell. The homeowners ran first to their neighbors, then to their telephones.

Moss took the calls, listening to one demand or suggestion after another as the buttons on his office telephone flashed impatiently.

The rats should be shot. The rats should be poisoned. What about the children? Would there be bubonic plague? What was going to be done about the god-damn plums? One man wondered if the trees could be gelded, like horses, so that they would produce blossoms but no fruit. Vyola Olinger felt the whole Plum Orchard ought to be declared a federal disaster area.

When Moss left his office, his brain was pinched and screaming. He had listened to so much talk about rats that he felt like one, trapped in a maze, running this way, then that, searching for an exit.

He drove his car home and, without entering the house, went into the garage. Wooden crates filled with plums lined one wall. He opened the door and backed his car up to the entrance and loaded it, stacking the trunk with boxes of fruit until he had to tie the lid shut, piling the seats and floor to the roof, leaving just a small space for him to drive. The Frazer sagged at the tail like a custom car of the 1950's. The engine labored against the added weight, then moved the dented vehicle forward, gathering momentum.

Moss turned onto the highway. Once it had served the orchards round it; now, flanked by car lots, drive-in restaurants, drive-in cleaners, even drive-in banks, it was the asphalt master. Still, somewhere along this route there must be a packing operation, a commercial outfit, a co-op, perhaps a small ranch-pack, that would take his plums. A road can't completely escape its past.

Moss drove so slowly that even in the right-hand lane people had to pull out and pass, cursing him. At every stop light he had to pump the brakes, then get the overloaded car off to a quivering start. Cars whooshed past him like jet aircraft; kids taunted him. The world became a blur.

He drove like this for more than forty miles, until the first fruit trees came into sight. It was nearly dark, so he followed the first dirt road next to the first rural mailbox until he came to a farmhouse where he asked about packing plants nearby. The farmer, a gaunt, leathery, suspicious man, maintained his own packing operation because he didn't know of another in the area. As if to prove he wasn't lying, he offered Moss a tour of his simple shed. There was no machinery, just tables, bins filled with plums and apricots, and empty field lugs. Not even a conveyor. Everything—grading, sorting, and packing—must be done by hand.

"Where do you get your help?" Moss asked.

"The lord's been good to me. I got eight kids."

"I see."

His pointed face and big, droopy ears made him look vaguely canine. He stared at Moss, waiting, except when he spoke. What was he hiding here?

"How would you like some more business?" said Moss.

"Got all I can handle."

"Suppose you got the fruit for nothing? Top-quality plums."

"Ain't interested. Mean I'd have to hire help. Can't afford it." He switched off the lights. "Don't like to waste the juice."

Moss followed him outside into the evening. A small boy, apparently wearing only overalls and badly in need of a haircut was peeking around a corner of the building.

"Git!" the farmer shouted savagely, and the boy ran off toward the house.

"Don't you even want to take a look at the fruit? I brought some with me."

"Nope."

"You can have it as a gift."

"Got all I need."

They walked over to Moss's car, and the farmer kicked a balding tire.

"No, I got a right-nice operation here. Just my size," he said.

"And you'd actually turn down a chance to increase your business?"

"You better believe it."

There, thought Moss, as he started the reluctant engine, was your true man of the soil, all stubborn, unreasoning integrity. He leaned out the window to say good-bye, but the farmer was off in the trees, where he had just flushed another urchin.

Just before he reached the junction of the farmer's dirt road and the highway, Moss stopped, turned off the lights and engine and unloaded all his cargo, stacking the lugs neatly alongside the byway. He felt guiltless. What was littering compared with child labor?

When he started the engine again and put it in gear, the car barely budged. He gave it more gas, and got only a thin, superficial sound. At last, by stomping the gas pedal to the floor, he persuaded the car to drag itself slowly forward. It drove worse empty than it had loaded; there was no power, and the temperature needle was up into the danger zone. Turning onto the highway, he clung to the shoulder and searched for a gas station.

In this disabled condition, he drove the longest two miles of his life, hating himself, his car, and his plum trees.

On pure inertia, the Frazer rolled into a grimy off-brand gas station, where a stringy, leering teen-age attendant examined its innards and pronounced it dead.

"You been draggin' with this heap, man?"

The boy told Moss that if he left the car there at the station, the manager might give him ten dollars for it as junk. Moss cleaned out the glove compartment and gave the boy his phone number. Then he crossed the highway, faced the traffic heading back the way he'd come, and stuck up his thumb.

To Moss, his old car had been his last link with youth, impulsiveness, idealism, freedom. He had imagined himself driving it until it became a curiosity. He'd move up the business ladder, but drive the same old car, obviously a lesser model than he could afford. It would be that one humanizing eccentricity that all first-rate men seem to have. Also, an example of innate thrift. Eventually, it would become an antique that Moss, white-haired like the old fruitgrower who had rejected Rancho Estates, would refuse to part with at any price. And now, the car had quit him, as if in disgust; and Moss's ambitions lay buried beneath an avalanche of plums.

Barbara saw him coming through the last small stand of fruit trees near the house, dragging his feet, his suit coat slung over one shoulder. At first she thought there'd been an accident, but as she studied his walk she knew he wasn't hurt physically, just down. And when she saw his dark, troubled face, her heart was moved.

For a long time, Barbara had waited for him to notice the change in her. Since the time when she realized that O'Malley was going to die she had known and tried to become what her husband needed. Patiently she had cared for their house and their baby and waited. When at last Moss realized that he needed her, she would be ready. And now she knew the time had come.

He walked inside, animated and complaining, replying to everyone at once. What did they want of him, for Chrissake? A man buys a lot with trees on it, and the trees are his. He's stuck with them, for better or for worse. The fruit was theirs when they wanted it; if there was too much now, that was their problem. You learn to live with trees; you don't return them to the manufacturer.

Quietly she agreed with him, then put the baby to bed while Moss stared, seething, out at the hated houses.

He mixed a pitcher of Martinis, poured one, and drank it. On an empty stomach, it felt like a sigh. Barbara joined him for the second one. Whatever was to be argued was already lost. Subdued by that fact, Moss turned upon himself.

"I wish that I could be a tougher man."

"I don't," Barbara disagreed gently.

"I've always known, deep down, that I was going to be left with nothing." He said this in a tone so despondent that there could be no reply. His "nothing" included everything and everyone.

So Barbara went silently into the kitchen to prepare dinner. As soon as she was out of his sight, she breathed deeply, and there was a shudder at the bottom of her breath.

They ate in silence, Moss morosely staring at his plate while Barbara served and watched him, searching for some communicative word or expression. There was none. And for a moment she wondered how he would look and what he would say if she simply told him, "Ray, I'm leaving you." It seemed as though he would not care or even hear.

She had cleared off the dishes and was rinsing them at the sink when she heard his voice behind her. "Leave them. Please. Let's go outside."

And in her apron she followed him out onto the porch into the darkness. Around them, the electric whirr of crickets rose as though it powered the lights. Somewhere a youngster practiced the scale on a trumpet, and dogs barked fearfully at the night.

"What I said before I didn't mean. I'm sorry."

They sat in old, unraveling wicker chairs, facing out at the trees, not quite side by side.

"To leave things like this is worse than destruction. It's half-assed. People will say that a planned community is impossible. They'll use this as an example to discourage anyone from trying it again. Or, even worse, they'll say it works, and there'll be bad imitations of a bad original."

They sat for minutes, weighing that, before Moss spoke again.

"I have to finish what I've started. Then someone can try again."

Barbara rose and came to him across the dark, warm and trembling, smelling of soap and kitchen grease, and he kissed her. He slid the cushion off the porch glider and tossed it flat on the floor. And then they lay down on it and made love as though all the times before —even the first time—had simply been practice.

When they left the porch, it was still warm outside and hushed. Overhead, thickly clustered stars were leaking light through the canopy of dark. Far below, the plum trees waited for another morning's sun.

Moss reported late to his office, wearing his old khaki trousers, work boots, and frayed hickory shirt. There were a dozen messages for him, and he threw them all away. Instead of returning calls, he placed one to the first heavy-duty gardener he found listed in the yellow pages, a Japanese. Then he walked outside and waited.

They arrived in a rusty pickup truck, the boss and two helpers, all Japanese, wearing baseball caps, with chain saws and double-edged axes and rope. And with a busy politeness they fell to work on the trees. The chain saws' steel teeth ripped into the trunks; their giant-insect whines tore the air.

Moss worked, too, swinging an ax. Awkwardly at first, until he found his timing and got the feel of the work. Then more smoothly, swinging the axe in an even plane, cutting the trunks into logs, splitting the branches into kindling, trimming away the fruit and leaves and bits of twig.

He pushed himself. His forearms ached and his palms blistered, and his clothes soaked through with sweat. Hands stinging, chips of wood flying up into his hair and eyes, he thought himself a machine, beyond fatigue, functioning until a breakdown.

They moved rapidly down the rows, across the lawns and through the parking lot, attacking the trees in twos, felling them with chain saws and lopping off the side branches. Whenever they'd cut enough to fill the truck, they loaded it, and two men drove the load away while the other two kept cutting.

People stopped to watch, distantly incredulous. Apparently, some order had been given. Those who recognized Moss stayed well clear of his ax's wide, destructive arc and his furious energy.

His blisters filled with water, broke, and ran; his limbs were stretched with strain. And yet he felt as though he worked with the body of another; numbed and then exhilarated, he escaped entirely from himself for the first time in years.

They kept at it all through the afternoon, working with growing weariness until the methodical Japanese began to glance hopefully toward Moss for some signal to quit. Finally, their boss suggested to Moss that they finish up in the morning, and Moss reluctantly agreed.

The gardeners packed up within minutes, fearing he would change his mind, and left him alone amid acres of open, emptied ground. He arrived home late for dinner and fell asleep at the table over plum cake.

In the morning he awoke before the baby and rose, painfully stiff, while Barbara slept. Ignoring breakfast, he dressed and hunted up a pair of work gloves in the garage to cover his sore, raw hands. And then he went outside and started on the trees again without waiting for the crew of gardeners.

He worked swiftly, heating up into a sweat despite the morning coolness, and soon the past day's stiffness drained from his limbs. The sun rose, and people stirred and glanced out their windows at him while shaving or eating breakfast. As the cars rolled from the driveways and headed slowly down the streets, the truck and the gardeners arrived; then they were at work again as though they'd never left.

At noon it was done. The last of the log-sized trunks and branches had been cut and carried off. Moss and the gardeners gathered up the loose leaves and small branches and built a fire in a large vacant lot. It was a long time starting, and it smoked at first, but they kindled the fire with paper and construction scraps until it blazed bright and hot. The men stood silently around it for a while, as if they needed to draw its warmth even though the sun was now in full heat overhead. And the sweet, sacrificial scent of burning fruit rose around them and hung in a still haze that covered the whole community.

The separation of person and place was now complete. The houses could be anywhere.

Moss paid the gardeners in cash, adding a bonus

to the agreed price. Bowing, they thanked him and left him alone to tend the fire, at his insistence. He chopped up pieces of leafy branch and added them to the flames until the last piece of the last plum tree had been turned to white, glowing ash. Then he shoveled earth over the remains. For a while it burned, too, and smelled a little like fresh bread. When the last ember winked out, Moss gathered up his tools and walked home.

Now I am free, for better or worse. Now I can begin anew. Or give up.

He called to Barbara as he entered the house and sat, in a slouch, on the living-room sofa. His hands were black with dirt and soot; there was sweat in every crease of his clothing. He waited, gathering the energy to undress and take a shower.

She came in carrying the baby and glanced at her husband's filthy weariness with surprise, then sympathy. She set the baby on the floor, and the child rested on its hands and knees and stared at the carpet.

"I'd like the coldest beer you have," he said.

"Watch her for a minute?"

"Sure," said Moss. And Barbara left the room.

Slowly the infant took notice of the world around her. She sighted along the carpet to the furniture, past the coffee table to the sofa. She saw Moss's dirty, booted feet, his stained and blackened pants and shirt, his sooty face, singed eyebrows, and matted hair. She looked at him and smiled. A small smile at first, widening as she stared. And Moss smiled back, his teeth flashing white against the dirt. For the first time, she recognized him.

The baby's smile became a laugh, and Moss, seeing himself in the baby's eyes, laughed, too. Seeing Moss laugh, the baby laughed louder. A dimple appeared in her cheek. Her laugh retreated to a smile, and Moss made a face, and the baby laughed again.

Moss got up and crossed the room and lifted the child up, his hands blackening her diaper and white cotton shirt, and looked into the laughing, trusting face. And then he hugged his warm, yeast-smelling daughter to him and began to do an awkward little dance around the room. He hummed a tune as he danced, and there were tears in his eyes.

I persevere, because life's possibilities will not subside.